*Lanie had the smile of an angel.
Achingly vulnerable.
Completely kissable.*

Garrett forgot for a second where they were or that Lanie was eight months pregnant. All he could think was that he wanted to kiss her, right then, right there. He couldn't recall the last time he'd wanted to kiss a woman this badly.

Why did she have this effect on him? Did the woman weave some sort of magic spell?

Garrett stared determinedly out the narrow window, watching the occasional car pass outside the doctor's office. He tried to think about a land development company he'd been considering buying for the Blakemore Corporation. He tried to think about his upcoming trip to Japan to consult on an overseas merger.

But no matter what he did, his mind kept drifting back to Lanie.

How would he feel if Lanie truly was his wife and she was having *his* baby...?

Dear Reader,

Silhouette Romance novels aren't just for other women—the wonder of a Silhouette Romance is that it can touch *your* heart. And this month's selections are guaranteed to leave you smiling!

In Suzanne McMinn's engaging BUNDLES OF JOY title, *The Billionaire and the Bassinet,* a blue blood finds his hardened heart irrevocably tamed. This month's FABULOUS FATHERS offering by Jodi O'Donnell features an emotional, heartwarming twist you won't soon forget; in *Dr. Dad to the Rescue,* a man discovers strength and the healing power of love from one *very* special lady. *Marrying O'Malley,* the renegade who'd been her childhood nemesis, seemed the perfect way for a bride-to-be to thwart an unwanted betrothal—until their unlikely alliance stirred an even more incredible passion; don't miss this latest winner by Elizabeth August!

The Cowboy Proposes...Marriage? Get the charming lowdown as WRANGLERS & LACE continues with this sizzling story by Cathy Forsythe. Cara Colter will make you laugh and cry with *A Bride Worth Waiting For,* the story of the boy next door who *didn't* get the girl, but who'll stop at nothing to have her now. For readers who love powerful, dramatic stories, you won't want to miss *Paternity Lessons,* Maris Soule's uplifting FAMILY MATTERS tale.

Enjoy this month's titles—and please drop me a line about *why* you keep coming back to Romance. I want to make sure we continue fulfilling *your* dreams!

Regards,

Mary-Theresa Hussey

Mary-Theresa Hussey
Senior Editor Silhouette Romance

Please address questions and book requests to:
Silhouette Reader Service
U.S.: 3010 Walden Ave., P.O. Box 1325, Buffalo, NY 14269
Canadian: P.O. Box 609, Fort Erie, Ont. L2A 5X3

THE BILLIONAIRE
AND THE BASSINET

Suzanne McMinn

Silhouette
R O M A N C E™
Published by Silhouette Books
America's Publisher of Contemporary Romance

To the best friends a writer could have—
Jill Shalvis and Mary Schramski.

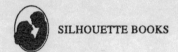 SILHOUETTE BOOKS

ISBN 0-373-19384-X

THE BILLIONAIRE AND THE BASSINET

Copyright © 1999 by Suzanne McMinn

Visit us at www.romance.net

Printed in U.S.A.

Books by Suzanne McMinn

Silhouette Romance

Make Room for Mommy #1191
The Bride, the Trucker and the Great Escape #1274
The Billionaire and the Bassinet #1384

SUZANNE McMINN

lives in a small Texas town. She always dreamed of being a writer, so she feels as if she's living in a fantasy these days. And with a real life including a husband, three young children and a scary mountain of laundry that seems to grow all by itself, she needs an active fantasy life to keep her going! She hopes her readers enjoy coming along for the ride. Suzanne loves to hear from readers and can be reached at: P.O. Box 12, Granbury, TX 76048.

Dear Reader,

Babies! I love babies. I love the way they blow bubbles and coo and laugh and spit up.... Oh, wait a minute, now I remember why I stopped having them. Seriously, I had three babies before I could shake off the baby lust. My two boys, Ross and Weston, are in elementary school, and my daughter, Morgan, is three. They aren't babies anymore, and maybe that's why I love writing about that stage of a child's life now. Babyhood passes swiftly, and sometimes it's hard to enjoy it while it's happening, because you are so tired from all those midnight feedings! Thank goodness for photographs to immortalize how they looked...and books to remember how it felt to love and cuddle them when they were little enough to fit into the crook of your arm. Whether you've already had your babies, or are still looking forward to that day in the future, I hope you enjoy reading *The Billionaire and the Bassinet,* and imagining along with me that special day when your newborn comes into your life. Ah! Babies...

Happy reading,

Suzanne McMinn

Suzanne McMinn

Chapter One

Lanie Blakemore opened her front door onto a sweet spring afternoon in Deer Creek, Texas and stared into a face she knew—and had never thought she'd see again.

Both a dazed numbness and a pulsing electricity hit her all at once. Was he real? A bizarre product of her imagination?

Around her the world sharpened. Bees buzzed merrily about the honeysuckle vines, their drone harmonizing with the flap of sheets from the back-yard clothesline. The sugary scent of the cookies she'd just taken out of the oven mingled with the fragrance of freshly mown grass, carried up the street by the light May breeze.

She tried to reach out, touch him, find out if he was real—but she couldn't. Her hands felt as if they belonged to someone else. Her heart hammered in her chest, deafening her to any other sound—to the birds chirping from their nest in the oak tree, to the distant hum of a car on the next street over, to the words coming out of the man's mouth as he stood in front of her.

"Ben?" she whispered, one hand grappling for the door frame, her knees soupy. Her other hand went instinctively to her swollen stomach.

The man was saying something to her. At least, she could see his mouth moving. She still couldn't hear him. A rushing sound filled her ears then, and in another second, everything went black.

Garrett Blakemore lunged forward, cursing, and scooped the woman in the doorway into his arms just before she struck the stoop. She felt surprisingly light, fragile.

It hadn't occurred to him that his resemblance to Ben would shock his cousin's widow to this extent. The last thing he'd meant to do was scare the living daylights out of her.

At least, he hadn't meant to scare the living daylights out of her *yet*.

Moving quickly inside the house, Garrett adjusted his grip on the unconscious woman. Along with the strong, sweet fragrance emanating from the back of the house came the more subtle scent of something soft and feminine. Something that reminded him of springtime and apple blossoms.

Something innocently alluring.

Garrett pulled his thoughts up short. What was wrong with him? The innocence of Ben's widow was definitely in doubt, and no amount of feminine allure could resolve that particular question.

What Garrett was after was proof. Hard, scientific evidence, one way or another, to show that Lanie had been telling the truth in the letter she'd sent. Ben's father, Walter Blakemore, needed the truth—and Garrett owed it to the uncle who'd raised him to help find it.

And he owed it to Ben.

Garrett crossed from the foyer to the parlor of the old house, worried about the woman's state of unconsciousness. Fainting couldn't be good for anyone, and she was pregnant—that was obvious enough. At least that part of her letter hadn't been a lie.

Garrett registered surprise at the contrast between the home's faded exterior and its bright interior as he gently placed the woman on one of the long couches and sat beside her on the edge. The cozy parlor wasn't what he'd expected.

Outside, a crumbling sidewalk led to a narrow front porch nearly consumed by unruly bushes. A worn sign stuck up from the midst of the scraggly lawn, its flowing pink letters announcing the home to be the Sweet Dreams Bed and Breakfast. The home itself looked to be about a hundred years old, with pink gingerbread trim decorating the flaking white wooden siding.

The inside presented a shining contrast. Soft

peach walls and plump contemporary-style couches
were set among gently aged antiques. Handwoven
rugs decorated the polished oak floor. A vase of
fresh-picked flowers cheered one corner. It was
comfortable and warm and very, very feminine.

Awkwardly Garrett patted Lanie's hand, hoping
for a response. She was young, he noticed as he sat
beside her. Probably about the same age Ben had
been. He'd seen her only once before, at Ben's funeral. She'd arrived as the service had begun and
had left the instant it ended. But he remembered
her—remembered the soft blond waves, the deli-
cately featured face, the mysterious eyes hidden behind dark glasses.

He remembered that she'd been the cause of so
much misery in his family for so many months.

She looked small and vulnerable now. Her body,
except for her swollen middle, seemed slender beneath the flowing T-shirt. And despite everything,
he couldn't help feeling a surge of some sort of
primal, protective instinct. The sensation was unfamiliar. And unwelcome.

Focusing deliberately on the problem at hand,
Garrett patted Lanie's hand again and called her by
name. She didn't move. He thought back to his first
aid training in college. He noted she wasn't wearing
anything constricting. The pink cotton shirt, with
its soft, scooped neck, flowed loosely to her hips,
with white, clingy leggings following the slender
line of her thighs and calves below.

Very shapely thighs and calves, narrowing down

to slim ankles and small feet encased in white tennis shoes.

Garrett swallowed, his gaze traveling back up her legs. Pregnant women weren't supposed to be sexy, were they?

He was tired. That had to be it. He'd sworn off women after his marriage—a short-lived debacle that had finished off whatever naive delusions about love and trust he might have once had.

Apparently, however, his libido was in rebellion, reacting to anything female that came within fifty yards, no matter how inappropriate. Garrett took a deep breath and forced his gaze from Lanie's shapely legs. He reached for one of the fat peach pillows tossed into a side chair and propped it beneath her ankles.

"Lanie?" he called again, softly. "Lanie?"

He ran a finger along her cheekbone, gently trying to rouse her. He wondered what color her eyes were, what had been hidden behind those dark glasses at the funeral. Minutes ago, when she'd opened the door, he'd barely had time to register anything at all. He hadn't noticed if her eyes were brown or blue—

Suddenly, as he dropped his hand from her jaw, her lashes fluttered, and he had his answer. She had the most beautiful blue eyes he'd ever seen, bigger than the Texas Hill Country sky and at least as mysterious. Slowly, cautiously, she focused her gaze on him.

"I'm sorry," he said quietly. "I didn't mean to frighten you. Are you all right?"

Lanie blinked, remembering where she was, remembering the man in front of her. The man that looked like Ben—but wasn't Ben.

She forced back tears. She'd thought, for just that one second—

"I'm fine," she managed, her mouth cottony. She struggled to sit up, but fell back again as black spots filled her vision and nausea choked her. She felt weak, boneless.

"Careful. Not so fast."

She noticed his voice. So like Ben's, yet different. It was deeper, harder, darker—like so many other aspects of the man, she realized, as her vision once again cleared.

The likeness to Ben was only superficial, she could see now. This man's hair was blacker and thicker than Ben's, his shoulders broader, his jaw more square, his lips more sensual, his eyes more penetrating.

Swallowing dryly, she felt uncharacteristically vulnerable. And very much alone.

He was a Blakemore. He had to be. No one could look this much like Ben and not be a Blakemore.

"Are you sure you're okay?" he asked, his gaze unrelenting. He'd been sitting beside her, but now he stood, towering over her. He was tall, solidly built, larger than Ben.

"I'm fine," Lanie said again, sounding feeble even to herself. She pushed herself up again, this time gingerly, until she came to a sitting position. Her body was starting to cooperate, thank goodness.

"I don't—I've never fainted before," she added self-consciously.

The episode embarrassed her. How long had she been out? How had she gotten from the back door to the couch? Of course he must have carried her. The thought of being held in the arms of this stranger made her incredibly uncomfortable.

She thought she remembered something, just as she came to—had that been his hand she'd felt on her cheek? All she remembered was the touch. The gentleness.

She frowned, bewildered by the clouded memory. Could this man with his hard mouth and cold eyes have touched her so tenderly? The skin of her cheek tingled with lingering awareness, confusing her further.

"Do you need to me to call a doctor for you?" he asked. His words were solicitous, but his demeanor remained impassive.

Lanie shook her head.

"I'm Garrett Blakemore." His serious, hard eyes never left hers. "And you're Lanie McCall, I take it?"

"Lanie Blakemore," Lanie said automatically, not surprised. Since when had the Blakemores ever accepted her as one of their own? She'd only faced Walter Blakemore once, at Ben's funeral. And the old man had coldly turned his back at her approach. A slap couldn't have been plainer.

She worked to place Garrett's name. Ben's cousin, she remembered quickly. She recalled that he and Ben had been close as children, but not so much as they'd grown older. The two had been raised like brothers after Garrett's parents had died in a plane crash. Garrett had fitted right into his uncle's empire of wealth, real estate and business holdings. He loved the power, the pressure, the hours and the travel. All the wheeling and dealing that Ben had detested had come naturally to Garrett.

"I'm here on behalf of Walter Blakemore," Garrett went on without acknowledging that she'd even spoken. "In regard to the letter you sent him."

Lanie froze, instantly alert. Months of inner turmoil had preceded the letter. Ben had described his father as controlling, domineering, powerful. But this baby was a Blakemore, and her conscience had left her no choice. Walter Blakemore had the right to know his grandchild. And her baby, already robbed of one parent, had the right to know his grandfather.

"The baby isn't due for another month," she pointed out. What could Walter Blakemore want with her now, before the baby was even born?

"Right. Well, there are several things that need to be settled, if you feel well enough to talk." Garrett arched a brow and waited.

"Settled?" Lanie's nerves went on red alert. "What do you mean, settled?" An unfamiliar bunching sensation moved across her lower abdomen. Instinctively she slid her hand over her stomach. Then the pain receded, and she refocused on the man before her.

He moved to sit down in one of the chairs across from the couch. "Do you mind?" he asked politely, and Lanie shook her head again.

He chose a hard-backed chair. It was Friday afternoon—a business day. He'd probably spent the morning in an Austin boardroom before making the hour's drive to Deer Creek, yet his shirt wasn't even wrinkled. Somehow, his ultrameticulous appearance only added to the daunting aura that surrounded him. He was a man accustomed to wielding power, to efficiently dictating to the world around him—and having it obey him.

"Walter is concerned about the baby's welfare," Garrett said abruptly. "He's worried about the baby being born in a rural area, where the medical care may be inadequate. He'd like to bring you to Austin—"

Lanie's eyes popped. Shock drummed through her bloodstream. "What?" She had no intention of going anywhere!

"He's prepared to provide you with a place to live, and the finest medical care until the baby is born. As you know, Ben was his only child, and if this is Ben's baby, it will be his only grandchild and heir—"

"*If* this is Ben's baby?"

"Of course," Garrett went on, not responding to Lanie's interruption, "paternity—and the child's rightful inheritance—can only be established by the appropriate blood and DNA testing which we will arrange to have performed at the time of the child's birth—''

"No!" Hurt, more than she'd thought possible, considering she barely knew Walter Blakemore, washed over Lanie. Just knowing anyone would even think she might lie about the baby being Ben's—for money, no less!—felt like a stab to the heart.

"According to your letter," Garrett carried on calmly, "you're now eight months pregnant— which is approximately the same amount of time that has passed since Ben's death." His cold eyes raked her. "I'm sure you can understand Walter's concerns."

"No. No, I can't."

Lanie pushed herself up from the couch heavily, her hips aching from the baby's weight. As she stood, another painful sensation, this time sharper and harder, spun out over her belly, and she bit down on her lip to keep from crying out.

Garrett stood as well. "I understand you're up-set—" He stopped short. "Are you all right?" He stared at her, and for the first time he didn't look quite so sure of himself.

"I'm fine," Lanie bit out. "I want you to leave. You can go back to Austin and tell Walter Blake-more—oh!" She couldn't speak as another agoniz-ing sensation rolled over her abdomen.

"What is it? What's wrong?" He sounded downright panicky now. Lanie felt the hysterical urge to laugh, but she was in too much pain.

"I don't know." She sank back down to the couch, shaky, wrapping her arms over her belly as the pain ebbed again. "I think—I think I might be in labor."

Chapter Two

"What did you say?" Garrett wanted Lanie to tell him he'd heard wrong.

She didn't.

"I think I might be in labor," she said again. Her voice shook and her pupils grew enormous.

Apprehension fingered up Garrett's spine. He wished he was back in Austin. He wished he was anywhere but where he was. He wasn't used to being around pregnant women. Especially pregnant women who said they were in labor. "I thought you said that you were only eight months along," he insisted.

"I *am* only eight months along," Lanie said quickly, her big eyes filled with anxiety. "It's too early! And Patty's out of town. I can't have the baby when Patty's out of town." She sounded really scared now.

Garrett blinked. "Who's Patty?"

"She's a friend. She's my birth coach." She twisted her hands in her lap.

Her obvious distress registered with Garrett. Suddenly whether Lanie carried Ben's baby or not didn't matter. All that mattered was that she was a human being who needed help.

And so did he. Emergency childbirth was not in his repertoire. Stocks and bonds, real estate and development, business mergers and takeovers—not babies. Definitely not babies.

"We need to get you to a doctor." And fast. Lanie looked like a terrified rabbit, and Garrett wasn't feeling much better himself.

"Yes." Lanie didn't move.

"Do you have a bag?"

She stared. "A what?"

"A bag. You know, a bag. To take to the hospital with you," he clarified impatiently.

They always had bags in the movies, didn't they? Garrett's thoughts hurtled along. In fact, he was starting to feel like one of those movie dads-to-be— as in, panicked. Only in the movies, the moms-to-be always seemed to know what they were doing, and in this case Lanie wasn't helping.

"I haven't packed one yet." Lanie stared at him. "You know, I might not even be in labor," she said abruptly. "I don't want to go to the hospital. Maybe it's false labor. I don't even feel anything now." She seemed to latch on to the idea, brightening.

False labor. Garrett had no idea what that was, but he wasn't taking any chances on ending up playing doctor in the parlor. She needed medical attention. He couldn't be responsible for any harm coming to her unborn child, even if it wasn't Ben's.

"You've fainted," he pointed out. "Shouldn't you at least let your doctor know about that?"

He heard the soft intake of her breath, watched her press her fingers to her lips. "You're right." She looked worried now.

Garrett took charge. Picking up the phone on the side table, he turned to her. "What's your doctor's number?" He checked his watch. He hoped her physician didn't leave early on Fridays.

Lanie reeled off the number automatically while Garrett punched it in. When it started ringing, he handed her the phone.

Garrett listened while Lanie asked for the nurse, then described the hardening and bunching in her abdomen and reported the fainting incident. She was silent for several moments, listening, before thanking the nurse and replacing the receiver.

"Well?"

"She told me not to worry, that fainting won't hurt the baby, but they may want to run a test for anemia. She thinks I should go ahead and come into the office so Dr. Furley can check me. As for the contractions, they might be false labor, but she wants to be sure."

Lanie felt silly already. So much for the poise with which she normally prided herself. A few isolated contractions, and she'd practically fallen apart. She didn't even want to think about the fainting episode. That hadn't been like her, either.

Annoyed, she stood up and retrieved her purse and keys from the kitchen. She nursed the tiny hope that when she came back to the parlor, Garrett would have taken the hint and decided to go back to Austin. She never wanted to see him again.

Unfortunately he was standing by the door waiting for her.

"Ready?" he asked. "My car's out front."

Lanie did a double take. "I've got my own car," she pointed out, stubborn now that the pain had gone. "I can drive myself. It's false labor. I'm sure." She felt perfectly fine now.

"You weren't so sure a minute ago," Garrett responded.

"I changed my mind." The last person Lanie wanted assistance from was the man who'd virtually accused her of lying about her baby's paternity. Now that she'd lost the edge off her fear, the anger at the Blakemores for doubting her word about Ben being the father of her baby returned full force.

"Well, I haven't changed *my* mind." Garrett stood his ground. "I'm not about to let you drive over there by yourself."

Lanie stared back at him, frustrated. She'd liked him better a few minutes ago when he'd looked flustered. Unfortunately he seemed to have recovered what she suspected was his usual arrogance.

"Your opinion doesn't matter," she informed

him coolly, slinging her purse strap over her shoulder, the keys in her hand jingling at the motion. "You were just leaving, as I recall. I can get five minutes across town to Dr. Furley's office on my own, thank you very much. I feel okay now. Really." She was starting to wonder if she'd imagined the severity of the contractions. She was stressed, that was all.

"I never said I was leaving. We still have business to settle—"

"No, we don't," Lanie said firmly, certain of at least that one thing. "That's where you're wrong. I'm not going to Austin with you, and I'm not the slightest bit interested in Walter's tests. He can accept or not accept the baby, it's his choice."

At this point, all she wanted was to have the Blakemores out of her life. She regretted sending the letter in the first place. All she'd wanted was for her baby to have a chance to know his father's family. But their reaction to her efforts wasn't only insulting—it was frightening.

What would they want next, once she'd complied with their demands for the tests? Would they demand she move to Austin, where Walter could dominate every aspect of her child's life?

She couldn't let Walter do to her baby what he'd done to Ben. She needed to get away from Garrett Blakemore, and think.

Problem was, he wasn't budging.

"I'm leaving now," she announced as she breezed past him toward the front door, "so you'll have to—oh!'' Pain—very real pain—gripped her lower abdomen again, pulling her up short.

"Lanie?" She felt Garrett come up behind her, supporting her as she bent forward. She grabbed her swollen middle, not realizing exactly when he slid his arm around her waist, only knowing that by the time the pain passed and her breathing returned to normal, he all but held her up. His arms were strong and secure…and gentle. So gentle. How could this hard man be so gentle?

She extricated herself from his support. He let go, but his eyes held hers. She saw gentleness there, too, then it was gone and his eyes were cold again.

"My car's out front," he repeated.

Tears stung at Lanie's eyes. She'd give anything if she didn't have to accept this man's help. She was afraid of giving him any power over her. She was afraid to need him. But she knew she had to think of her baby, put her baby first.

The pain of the last contraction had receded, but there were no two ways about it now. She could really be in labor, and she was scared.

Blowing out a frustrated breath, she moved to the door. "Okay. You can drive me." She blinked back the tears and met his gaze head-on. "But right after that, you're leaving."

The general practitioner's office, located in a small, one-story professional building, was neat and modern, at least from what Garrett could see of the place. A harried-looking woman stood writing out a check at the receptionist's counter, several toddlers clinging to her knees. Another patient, a white-haired lady who looked like she could have been in her early eighties, sat flipping through a women's magazine. She glanced up and smiled as she observed Lanie's condition.

After the mother and toddlers left, Lanie spoke to the receptionist while Garrett sat down. He noticed how, from the back, Lanie didn't even look pregnant. The lines of her figure were slim as a teenager's—long legs, slender hips, fragile-looking shoulders.

When she'd looked at him with pain, her eyes so huge and vulnerable, Garrett had wanted to just wrap her up somehow and promise her everything would be all right. It was a reaction that made no sense. Garrett crossed his arms and stared at Lanie as she came toward him and settled in the empty seat beside him.

"It'll be just a minute," she said.

"How are you feeling?" The one thing he was sure she wasn't faking was the pain. The terror on her face back at the house had been real.

"I'm fine. No more contractions." She smiled shakily, and Garrett realized two things. One, that she was a lot more relieved to be at the doctor's office than she'd been letting on.

And two, that she had the smile of an angel. Achingly vulnerable. Completely kissable.

Garrett forgot for a second where they were or that Lanie was eight months pregnant. All he could think was that he wanted to kiss her, right then, right there. He couldn't recall the last time he'd wanted to kiss a woman this badly. It was insane.

Why did she have this effect on him? Was this the effect she'd had on Ben? Did the woman weave some sort of magic spell?

She picked up a magazine from the table on the other side of her and began perusing the table of contents. Garrett leaned back, blankly studying the painting of a mother and child in a field of brilliant bluebonnets on the wall opposite them.

Bewitchment would certainly explain the irrational behavior that had characterized the last months of Ben's life. Ben had given up everything—his position in his father's company, his home, wealth, even his very place in the Blakemore family. All for a pretty little innkeeper he'd rearended at a traffic light and married a month later—against his father's orders.

Walter had cut Ben off in an effort to bring his son to his senses. Unfortunately there hadn't been time. An aneurysm had claimed Ben's life within six months of the marriage. He'd died without ever speaking to his father again. Or to Garrett.

It was still hard for Garrett to believe Ben was gone. Ben had been so full of life.

And he'd been young—even naive, perhaps. He could have been easy prey for a con artist.

Garrett snapped his gaze to Lanie, sitting quietly beside him. She was no sorceress, he reminded himself fiercely. This was no magic spell she weaved.

She was a con artist, plain and simple. The shocked innocence she'd put on when he'd broached the testing of the baby was part of her act. If the baby wasn't Ben's, if all she'd ever wanted from the second she'd latched on to Ben was a piece of the Blakemore fortune, she was hardly going to admit it right off the bat. He couldn't let big eyes and a sweet smile deter him from his purpose.

"Lanie Blakemore?" the nurse called.

Lanie stood, then disappeared through the door into the inner office.

Garrett stared determinedly out the narrow window, watching the occasional car pass outside the doctor's office. He tried to think about a land development company in New York he'd been considering buying for the Blakemore Corporation. He tried to think about his upcoming trip to Japan to consult on an overseas merger.

But no matter what he did, his mind kept drifting back to Lanie.

What if he was wrong, what if Walter was wrong? What if Lanie was innocent?

And then he had to wonder if she was really a sorceress, after all.

After what seemed like an eternity, he checked his watch, frustrated. Where was she? Was she really in labor? What was going on? He wanted to pace, but the idea sounded too corny, so he stayed put.

"Is this your first?"

Garrett looked up. The elderly lady across the

waiting room watched him. Her cheeks were pink and lined, her eyes bright with curiosity.

"Excuse me?"

"You and your wife must be very excited. It looks like that baby will be here soon." She smiled.

His *wife?*

Garrett stared at the elderly woman. It took him a full minute to realize she was actually talking about him and Lanie.

How would he feel if Lanie were his wife and she was having his baby? *Proud* was the first word that popped into Garrett's mind.

Then he thought about Vanessa. He and Vanessa had discussed having children, once or twice. That was as far as things had gotten.

That was as far as their marriage had gotten before Garrett had figured out that he'd been the biggest chump on planet Earth. Nothing like finding your wife in bed with another man to drive home the fact that trust was for idiots.

He wasn't going to make that mistake again. Not with anybody. And for sure not with Lanie. She might have eyes like a newborn foal's, but Garrett wasn't going to be taken in that easily.

"That's not my wife," Garrett said suddenly, sharply. "In fact, I barely know her." A fact he'd be well advised to remember, he added to himself.

The older woman looked startled.

Garrett picked up a newspaper from the table next to him and held it in front of his face, discouraging any further communication. He struggled to concentrate on the black-and-white print. And he wondered why he hadn't told Walter to send his sixty-year-old, stuffed-shirt personal attorney, Richard Houseman, on this little mission to Deer Creek.

"Now, remember, rest tonight, Lanie. And try not to worry."

Lanie thanked the nurse as she slipped through the door between the inner and outer offices. Her gaze went straight to Garrett. He folded up the newspaper he held and dropped it on the table, standing as she approached.

"Are you all right?" he asked immediately.

"I'm fine." Really, she wasn't. She was worried sick. The examination's conclusion was uncertain. Her pains had been erratic and had emanated from her lower abdomen rather than her back, leading Dr. Furley to suspect it was merely false labor. However, he had also reminded her that everyone's experience was different, and she could well be exhibiting very early labor, after all. Only time would tell.

Dr. Furley had reassured her that the baby was healthy and big enough to be born, and had performed another sonogram to reassure her. Still, Patty wouldn't be back until Sunday night. Lanie was scared to death of going through labor without her coach.

"You're sure you're fine?" Garrett probed. He looked suspicious, as if he didn't quite believe her.

"Yes, of course."

She made an appointment with the receptionist

for a regular prenatal visit the following week, determined not to tell Garrett any details. She wasn't going to have this baby before at least Sunday night, that was all there was to it, and she had no intention of sharing the doctor's warnings with Garrett. The information might up the coercion level for getting her to go back to Austin with him immediately, and as vulnerable as she felt, she didn't think she was up to the confrontation.

She had to admit she was glad to have him there to drive her home, though. She was definitely feeling a little weak and shaky. And thankfully, he seemed to have accepted her assurances. He was quiet as he escorted her out to the car again.

Starting up the engine, he turned to look at her. "Nothing's wrong? What about the pain you were having?" Garrett didn't move the car as he waited for Lanie to answer.

So much for accepting her word for anything.

"I told you, I'm fine," Lanie repeated, working to make her voice firm. Garrett's piercing dark gaze, so much like Ben's—and yet so different, unsettled her. She wasn't used to having anyone worrying about her.

For just a moment Garrett's attention and concern felt nice. Kind of warm and fuzzy, with just the right dash of the unknown.

Ben had certainly never worried about her. He'd always been too busy worrying about himself, angry and obsessed by his bitter emotional struggle with his father.

How would Walter Blakemore feel if he knew he was right about at least one thing about her—that his son's marriage to her had been a mistake?

Reality reared up, ugly and painful. The Blakemores hated her. Garrett wasn't worried about her. His concern and attention was not for *her*. He was worried about the possible Blakemore heir.

"It was just false labor, like I thought," she forced herself to say blithely. "Now, please, I really have to get home. I have guests coming in tonight."

She remembered suddenly she didn't even have the room made up. Just thinking of the evening ahead made her bone weary. She'd had a full house the night before—and had intended them to be her last guests for a while. She'd taken care not to allow bookings for the month preceding her due date and for six weeks afterward, the most time she could afford to close the struggling B&B. But she'd been feeling chipper this morning when a couple had called for last-minute reservations.

She regretted the impulse that had made her accept the booking. She wasn't feeling nearly so chipper now.

Garrett backed the car out of the parking space, but he wasn't through with his questions.

"How do you know it's false labor?" he asked as he swung the car into the street, heading in the direction of the B&B.

"The contractions were erratic," Lanie explained briefly. "And they went away. Also, the pain began in my lower abdomen, rather than my lower back—

which is where real contractions usually start." She looked out the window, as if intensely interested in the scenery passing by, discouraging further conversation. She had no intention of elaborating.

They passed through the town square, complete with a courthouse surrounded on four sides by active businesses that clearly appealed to Hill Country tourism—a hotel, several restaurants and antique and novelty shops. In a few minutes they arrived at the Victorian B&B. Lanie unhooked her seat belt and shoved open the passenger-side door.

"Thank you for taking me to the doctor."

"No problem." Garrett removed his keys from the ignition.

"I'm sorry you made this trip out here for nothing," she said with almost painful civility. "I really don't think there's anything else for us to talk about."

"Lanie—"

"I'm not going back to Austin with you," she said, cutting Garrett off. "And I don't even want to discuss those tests."

"Lanie—"

"Walter can believe whatever he wants to believe. I merely felt it was my duty to inform him about Ben's child. That's all. I don't want anything from him—not his help, and certainly not his money, if that's what he's afraid of. Tell him he can relax."

Salty pinpricks stabbed at Lanie's eyes. *What a time to get hormonal!* she cursed inwardly, determined to put the emotion down to her pregnancy rather than to the idea that she might give a hoot about what Ben's father thought. Or Garrett, for that matter.

"Lanie—"

"Goodbye," she managed, and got out of the car. She slammed the car door shut, wishing she could make a more graceful departure than that of a lumbering elephant, which was what she felt like at the moment.

She heard Garrett's car door shut behind her and knew he'd gotten out, too. "Lanie, I'm not leaving. Not tonight, at least."

Lanie's shoulders drooped at Garrett's words. She stopped in the middle of the street and swiveled to face him, wishing desperately that he would disappear. She was far too tired to deal with him.

"Look, I'm not going to press you about the tests. Not tonight." Garrett approached Lanie. She looked tired, and he knew the decision he'd just come to was the right one. Her golden waves shifted in the wind as she stood there, the long tresses swinging softly around her small shoulders. The afternoon sun caressed her bare cheeks, the warm light loving her smooth skin. Again Garrett experienced an oddly protective sensation.

He put it down to the fact that the baby Lanie carried might be Ben's. This was about the baby, he reminded himself. Not Lanie.

"I heard what the nurse told you," he went on. "You're supposed to rest—and you have guests coming. I could stay and help.'' He didn't know what work this would entail, but he couldn't see leaving her alone right now.

He wasn't entirely convinced she was telling him everything about her visit with the doctor. Besides, nothing had been settled. He had to find out the truth, for Walter's sake. For Ben's sake.

And for his own, he realized abruptly. He had to know if Lanie was an innocent—or a liar. He didn't even want to think about why that was suddenly so important to him. It simply was.

Lanie blinked. ''You—help?''

She looked so shocked he didn't know whether to laugh or be insulted. He was getting tired of her looking at him like he was Attila the Hun.

Not that he cared whether she liked him or not. Not at all. It was just that as long as she disliked him this intensely, he was going to have a hard time getting her to cooperate.

He gave her what he hoped was a reassuring smile. ''Of course I can help. Why not?''

SUZANNE McMINN

Chapter Three

Lanie noticed Garrett looked kind of nice when he smiled. Less like a power broker, and more like a human. He even had a dimple, just on the left side, which she hadn't noticed before. Perhaps because the man didn't seem to smile all that much.

"I don't think it's a good idea for you to stay here tonight." As tempting as his help sounded, she didn't think having Garrett around, any more than necessary, would be a good idea at all. He hadn't been in town five minutes before he'd started trying to take charge of her life—demanding tests on the baby, commanding her to go to Austin and live under the Blakemores' thumbs until the baby's birth, insisting he drive her to the doctor's office.

Of course, driving her to the doctor's had been a good idea, but none of the rest of it was. She didn't want the Blakemores running her life—or worse, taking control of her baby.

"It's a great idea," Garrett persisted. "You need to rest, and I need a place to stay."

"You could drive back to the city," Lanie pointed out, pushing back the temptation he offered.

Help sounded awfully good, whether she wanted it to or not. She was just so tired.

She pulled herself together. "It's not that far to Austin," she dismissed. She turned her back on him and his help, trudging up the walk.

He came up behind her. "Are you always this stubborn?" he asked.

"Stubborn! Me?" Lanie stopped long enough to cast Garrett an arch look as he reached her side. "You're the one who can't take no for an answer."

She arrived at the front door and scoured her handbag for her housekeys. She found them, then immediately proceeded to drop them on the ground.

Garrett started to retrieve the keys for her, but Lanie knelt, awkwardly, and snatched them before he could.

"Please leave me alone." Tears stung at the back of her eyes again. Bending wasn't her best event these days, but she shook off Garrett's arm as he tried to help her straighten.

She felt as if she were teetering on the edge. Her exhaustion combined with the stress of the afternoon had been too much, and the last thing she wanted to do was break into one of those sudden bouts of hormonal tears that had plagued her throughout her pregnancy—right in front of Garrett.

She fumbled with the key, wiggling it into the hole, struggling with the old lock. Blinking back traitorous tears, she gratefully pushed the door open. A few more seconds and she could shut it in his face.

"Are you crying?"

She tried to ignore him as she moved through the doorway. He stuck his foot in the door and prevented her from closing it.

She didn't want to look at him, but he reached out and turned her face toward him, the touch strong and gentle at the same time. Lifting her eyes, she met his reluctantly. She dashed a hand at the moisture on her cheeks and lifted her chin a notch.

"You *are* crying." He sounded confused. He dropped his hand from her face, but not his stare. "Look, I don't know if this is pride or stubbornness or just that you don't like me much." An odd, almost painful light flickered in his eyes for a second, then disappeared. "But I think you need some help tonight." His voice was soft. "Will you let me stay?"

Lanie thought about going to the backyard and dragging the sheets off the line, hauling them upstairs and making up the bed, then greeting the guests with the customary refreshments. Her feet, her knees, her hips—every place where the baby's weight put unaccustomed pressure—ached like she

carried a two-ton truck instead of a tiny human being.

She wanted nothing more than to drop into bed
and let someone help her. But it wasn't safe for
Garrett Blakemore to be that someone. She knew
that.

But she said, "All right," anyway.

Garrett knocked lightly on the closed door to
Lanie's bedroom. "Lanie?"

"Come in," she called.

He poked his head around the doorjamb in time
to see her sitting up in bed, a fat pillow propped
behind her back. She was still dressed, her long legs
stretched out on a colorful quilt decorated in a pat-
tern of interlocking rings. A white lace curtain blew
softly at the open window, bringing the warm afternoon inside.

Despite the obvious reluctance with which she'd
agreed to let him help her out for the evening, she'd
acquiesced with surprising ease when he'd insisted
she go straight upstairs to rest. He knew this was
more likely an indication of the true state of her
exhaustion than any sign of surrender on her part.

She'd given him brief instructions about making
up two rooms with sheets from the line outside, and
had explained where to find the refreshments she
had prepared. She'd asked him to call her when the
guests arrived so she could come down to greet
them. But before he tended to any of the other prep-
arations, he'd decided to fix her something to eat.

"I brought you a sandwich and a glass of milk," Garrett said. He came around the side of the antique spool bed and placed a tray on the end table near her. Her wary gaze never left him. "And some cookies." He held out the glass of milk.

"You shouldn't have done that." Surprise widened her eyes as she took in the tray.

"Of course I should have," Garrett said. Her aversion to his assistance was really starting to annoy him.

He kept holding out the glass, and she finally took it, her slender fingers lightly brushing his in the exchange. A small electrical charge zinged up Garrett's arm, filtering through his irritation.

He backed up slightly in reaction, putting a little distance between himself and Lanie. It was just the oddness of being in her bedroom, he told himself. The situation was overly intimate, considering they'd only known each other a few hours.

"I don't want you waiting on me," Lanie protested. She set the glass down on the tray.

Garrett shrugged. "It's just a little something to eat. It's not a big deal. You need to keep up your strength."

She looked wan, and he didn't like it. He didn't like how it made him feel. He didn't like how he was worrying about this woman he'd only just met and had no reason to trust or even like.

Of course, he reminded himself, he did have one good reason for caring. The sooner she rested up, the sooner he could tackle the business at hand—

getting her to agree to come back to Austin with him. He worked to focus on the reason he was in Deer Creek, and to forget how pale and defenseless Lanie looked, propped in bed, surrounded by all this soft lace and patchwork simplicity.

The scene was a false picture, making her seem more maternal than small-town schemer. The whole setup was what was throwing him off balance, he decided. The sooner he got out of her bedroom, the better.

He strode to the door, determined to get the sheets and make up the guest rooms. And put as much distance as he possibly could between himself and Lanie's sweet, vulnerable eyes.

"Garrett?"

He stopped in the doorway and turned to look at her. She chewed her lip, hesitating, the glow from the sunset lighting her fine features. Her hands moved over the rounding of her belly in a seemingly unconscious gesture.

Garrett's gaze followed the movement of her hands, lured by the slow caressing motion that spoke of tender care for her unborn child. He wondered if the baby was moving, what it would feel like to place his hand there and feel the tiny life inside her kick....

He jerked his attention back to her face. "What?" he prompted curtly. He really needed to get out of her bedroom.

"I—uh..." She glanced at the tray, then back at him. She bit her lip again. "Thank you," she said finally, as if the words came with great difficulty. "I hope I didn't sound rude. I didn't mean to."

She sounded so sincere. Her hand moved over her stomach again. The light from the window settled around her like a halo.

Garrett swallowed tightly. "No problem," he answered, and made good his escape.

Lanie watched Garrett through her open window as he crossed the backyard, heading for the clothesline. The curtains fluttered about as the light breeze infused a warm, comfortable breath of fresh air into the room. She took a big gulp of it. She needed it. She needed something, anyway—something to stop her from making a complete and total fool of herself.

She felt touched by Garrett's thoughtfulness in bringing her supper. He'd even brought her cookies. It was such a simple yet considerate gesture. The sort of gesture she wouldn't have expected from the hard, cold businessman who'd all but accused her of trying to defraud his uncle.

Lanie tensed at the thought. The whole thing was so insulting. Why was Garrett really so intent on helping her this evening? Out of the goodness of his heart?

Fat chance of that! She blew out a frustrated breath. His help—and his suppers—were part of his plan to manipulate her into going back to Austin with him.

She should have thrown the supper tray right back in his face.

She eyed the meal in front of her. She was hungry, and she didn't see anything to be gained by not eating. After all, she'd need her strength if she was going to resist his power plays.

And there was no point wasting perfectly good cookies, was there?

Picking up the sandwich first, she took a bite and narrowed her gaze on her adversary. He'd rolled his sleeves up and begun tearing sheets down.

The muscles of his arms flexed in the sun as he reached upward. Lanie stared for long seconds before swallowing the bite of sandwich, then forcibly ripped her gaze from the sight in her yard. She took a swig of cold milk. Really, what was wrong with her? She was practically ogling the man.

She couldn't believe now she'd ever mistaken him for Ben. He was nothing like Ben. It was more than the subtle physical differences. There was something so serious, so earnest about Garrett.

Ben had been funny and exciting—in the beginning. They'd had a whirlwind courtship. He'd dared her out of her quiet life. *Her quiet rut,* as her grandmother who'd raised her used to say. She'd known Ben was marrying her over his wealthy father's objections, but he was determined and had insisted his father would come around. He said he wanted to get married and help her rebuild the bed-and-breakfast business she'd recently inherited after her grandmother's death.

Even though her grandmother was gone, Lanie could still hear her nagging. *Life is short, live while you're young, let your heart lead you.*

And in a moment of uncharacteristic spontaneity, Lanie had let her heart lead her. She'd married Ben.

The disillusionment had come quickly. Walter Blakemore couldn't accept his son's abrupt marriage, or his decision to leave the family business. He'd underscored his unbending resolve by cutting Ben off financially. But that hadn't been the worst of it. It was only after they'd married that Lanie finally understood what Ben's power struggle with his father was all about. He wanted his father's love—and no matter how much love she gave him, it could never be enough, never make up for what his father had withheld from him his entire life.

Ben had grown distant and morose, alternating between long silences and angry outbursts. And Lanie knew she'd made a mistake—that they had *both* made a mistake. But she wasn't a quitter and she'd tried to make their marriage work despite the coldness with which he'd pushed her away.

By the time he died, she wasn't sure if Ben had ever loved her or if she had merely been a means to break away from his father. But whatever the fate of their marriage might have been if he'd lived, she still mourned him—that his life had been cut too short, that her baby would never know its father.

She had little family of her own left—only a brother on military duty overseas. But Ben had family, and so did her baby.

Her gaze moved out the window again. The yard was empty now, the clothesline bare. Garrett was gone, which was just as well. She didn't need to be tempted by his strong arms, to fantasize what it would feel like to have those arms around her, to feel that exciting ripple of warmth inside her when he looked at her. Not when she felt so very lonely.

Thoughts of Garrett were dangerous. *Garrett* was dangerous. He was the sort of man who would have everything he wanted, wouldn't settle for less.

And he wanted something from her.

This time, Lanie couldn't hide from the little ripple that shuddered inside her. This time it was fear.

"Your home is lovely."

Garrett opened his mouth to explain to the Berringers, Lanie's guests for the night, that the Sweet Dreams Bed and Breakfast wasn't his home, but a soft voice from behind stopped him.

"Thank you."

He turned. Lanie, dressed now in a flowing yellow sundress that lit up her eyes and hair, seemed to float into the parlor. She smiled at the Berringers, looking rested and relaxed.

Weren't pregnant women supposed to be awkward? Garrett thought. There was nothing ungainly about Lanie.

She moved like a feather. A delicate, beautiful feather. Garrett found her gracefulness annoying.

But then, he found her mere presence annoying, he decided. He hadn't meant to call her down when her guests arrived—despite her instructions. He'd intended to avoid her entirely for the rest of the evening. But here she was, anyway.

"I hope you had a nice trip," Lanie was saying. She still hadn't looked at him.

He, on the other hand, was having a hard time taking his eyes off her.

"Oh, yes," Mrs. Berringer replied. She was a heavyset woman and the sofa made a groaning noise when she sat down on it. "But I'm so glad to be here."

She reached for one of the canapés artfully arranged on a tray on the coffee table. Garrett had placed the tray of appetizers out, just as Lanie had instructed.

Mr. Berringer settled into an armchair.

"Can I get you something to drink?" Lanie indicated a bottle of wine chilling in a bucket near the canapés. Another tray held several glasses.

The Berringers accepted, and Lanie sat down, leaning forward to pour the wine into the glasses. Garrett watched her long hair fall over her bare shoulders in shimmery, touchable waves. Unbidden came the urge to reach out, to wrap a finger around one of those locks, to discover just how soft and touchable they really were....

Garrett's chest tightened, and he realized he'd almost forgotten to breathe. This whole domestic setup was doing a number on his brain, he told himself. Either that, or she was, indeed, a sorceress.

"I'll take these things upstairs," he announced abruptly.

He grabbed the bags and bounded up the creaking, narrow stairs. When he came back down, he found Mrs. Berringer stuffing a canapé into her mouth and Lanie in the middle of what sounded like a history of the house.

"Then after my grandmother died, I took over the business," she was saying. "The house was in bad shape, and my grandmother had let the business slide in her later years. I was too attached to the house to leave it, since it's been in my family from the time it was built, around the turn of the century. I couldn't bear to let it go. It's very much a work-in-progress at this point. The exterior of the house still needs a lot of attention, and not all of the interior rooms have been restored. But I'm hoping to get another guest room opened soon so I can be at full capacity."

Garrett stood near the fireplace. He listened, watching Lanie sitting there in her sunshine dress with her golden waves, her foal eyes and her big smile as she talked about the house she obviously loved.

She seemed so genuine. So innocent.

Could she really be the scheming con artist Walter believed her to be?

Garrett cocked his head, frowning, frustrated by the opposing images in his head. She was responsible for tearing a son from his father. He shouldn't let himself forget that.

"The two of you must be very proud," Mr. Berringer said to Lanie. The older man swiveled his head around to take in Garrett. "Home renovation is hard work."

Garrett arched a brow at Lanie. Obviously the Berringers had assumed *he* was Lanie's husband. He expected her to disillusion them immediately.

"Yes, it is," she agreed simply. She raised her gaze from Mr. Berringer, but she didn't look at Garrett. He followed the direction of her study as it swept past him.

He turned his head toward the mantel over the fireplace. A small framed picture of Ben and Lanie stuck out from amidst the brass candleholders and knickknacks positioned there.

It wasn't a formal picture. Instead, the photograph showed a casual, sunlit scene, Ben and Lanie walking together barefoot on a beach, hand in hand, staring at each other, their eyes shining.

Garrett couldn't take his gaze off the photo. He only turned when he realized the Berringers were speaking to him, asking him something.

"What?" he asked.

"We were just wondering where a good place to eat around here was," Mr. Berringer repeated. He was standing now. Mrs. Berringer lumbered up behind him.

Garrett shook his head. "I don't—"

"There's a lovely, intimate little restaurant on the town square," Lanie said, rising as well, using her arms to push herself up, the strain in her face revealing the effort involved in mobilizing her burdened frame. Garrett barely resisted helping her. She wouldn't want his help, and he knew it. "It's quite historic, and the food is wonderful."

"That sounds like just the ticket." Mr. Berringer smiled back. He took his wife's arm. "I believe we'll just freshen up a bit and be off to the restaurant. We'll see you in the morning."

"I'll show you to your room," Lanie offered and led the way upstairs. She continued her discourse on the house, pointing out the octagonal-shaped stained-glass window at the foot of the stairs. "That's original to the home. The design was created by my great-grandmother..." Her voice filtered away as she mounted the stairs.

Garrett paced the parlor, thinking about Ben and Lanie, and the picture with shining eyes.

The image was out of sync with the impression Walter had painted. Walter was certain Lanie was out for a piece of the Blakemore fortune, that she'd snared Ben for the sole purpose of gaining the money he could one day inherit. That it was she who had prevented Ben from returning to the fold, and when he'd died and she'd lost her ticket to the Blakemore wealth, she'd come up with a pregnancy to get it back.

Hadn't money been what Vanessa had wanted in the end? What proof did Garrett have that Lanie didn't want the same thing?

Even though Vanessa had been the one to break their vows, Garrett's wife had been all too quick to hire a high-powered divorce lawyer and take the biggest settlement she could get.

Why should Lanie be different, despite her assertions of not wanting anything from the Blakemores? Her facade of innocence could be nothing but a smokescreen. After all, renovations had to be costly, and this old house still needed a lot of work. A lot of money.

With a baby—a baby she claimed to be a Blakemore heir—she held the key to the treasure, didn't she?

If she was telling the truth, that would be. As long as she refused to submit the child to testing, it would remain an *if*.

Not knowing whether or not he did have a grandchild, Walter would have no peace. And neither would Garrett.

The scent of springtime and apples teased into his thoughts, and he turned, knowing she was there even before he saw her. She said nothing to him, heading straight for the tray of refreshments. She picked it up.

"They thought I was your husband," Garrett said quietly.

Lanie straightened, tray in hand. "I know."

"Why didn't you tell them I wasn't?"

She gave a nearly imperceptible shrug of one bare shoulder. "It didn't seem important. Why explain? They won't be here long." Her gaze squared on his.

And neither will you.

He could almost hear her add that last line in her thoughts.

"I appreciate your help tonight" was what she did say. She shifted her weight from one foot to the other. "I hope you have a good night's sleep and a safe trip back to Austin in the morning." Her voice was dismissive yet polite. "Good night." She turned away, moving toward the kitchen.

He looked back at the photograph on the mantel.

"Wait," he said.

She stopped, pivoting slowly. She stared at him.

He picked up the photograph, studying it again for a long moment before lifting his gaze to her.

"When was this picture taken?"

"After we were married, we drove down to the Gulf. We spent a weekend there, our honeymoon."

A cloud of unreadable emotion shuttered her eyes. He wondered what she was thinking, remembering. Feeling.

He waited another long minute. "Why did you marry him?" he asked her suddenly.

He didn't think she was going to respond. He held his breath, an ache inside begging for the truth—and wondering if he'd know it if he heard it.

"I loved him," she said finally, almost on a whisper. And then the only sound in the room was the soft whoosh of the swinging kitchen door as she disappeared.

Garrett stared after her, then down again at the

photograph. He wasn't sure how long he stood there before he realized the fact of what he felt—suddenly, illogically—toward his cousin.

Envy.

Chapter Four

It was not much more than a breath, a sharp intake of air, but the sound from outside his door roused him from the floating half sleep he'd been in for most of what had seemed like a long, long night.

Garrett fumbled in the predawn pitch-black of his room for the lamp switch on the nightstand, blinking in the bright glare when he found it. He'd been unable to rest well and deep, not sure whether to place the blame on the unfamiliar surroundings or the proximity of the beautiful, mysterious Lanie.

But he did know by the soft sound he'd heard coming from her, that something was wrong. That he was in some strange, unwanted way tuned in to a woman he didn't even trust.

Swinging his legs off the side of the bed, he stood and strode to the door across the polished wood floor. He opened it quickly, the shaft of light slicing outward into the hallway.

Lanie leaned against the wall near the stairs in a long white gown, her hands splayed over her middle. Her glossy hair spilled around her, shielding her face as she bent forward.

"Lanie? What's wrong? Is it the baby?" Panic pounded through Garrett's veins. He rushed to her, slipped his arm automatically around her back, tried to bring her to an upright position.

"No, don't, I can't move right now," she whispered, her voice taut.

Garrett let go of her, feeling at a loss for what to do next. "Should I call the doctor?" he questioned nervously after a minute.

She looked up at him finally, her eyes huge and dark, her face ashen. "It's passed. It's nothing. I'm all right."

"It didn't look like nothing to me." It had looked like horrible pain to him. And he hated seeing her in pain; he instinctively wished he could soothe it.

He was a problem solver in his daily business, accustomed to stepping into a situation, making decisions, ordering strategy. He couldn't do anything about Lanie's pain. And it made him feel uncomfortably inadequate and lost.

"Dr. Furley said I might have erratic contractions, that it doesn't mean anything unless it keeps up. This is just more false labor."

She crossed her arms, the movement causing the

neckline of her gown to gape and the soft-looking mounds of her breasts to press upward. The tantalizing shadow of cleavage deepened, and he caught himself staring.

"Are you sure?" he managed to ask, focusing on her pale face, wishing he could believe his mind was this rattled because of lack of rest—not because of the vision of Lanie's generous curves. He wasn't a man who leered at women, and he was more than a little ashamed of himself because that was exactly what he'd just done. And she was pregnant to boot, for Pete's sake.

"Yes," she answered. "I'm fine, really. Please go back to bed. I'm sorry if I woke you."

"I wake early, anyway," he insisted. "What are you doing up?"

"This is a bed and *breakfast*. Get it?" She quirked a brow.

He smiled. He could see she'd gotten her attitude back, so he figured she had to be telling the truth about feeling better.

"Well, I'm awake. You might as well put me to work. What can I do to help?" She might be feeling better again, but it bothered him to think of her working. He noticed the subtle purplish shadows beneath her eyes.

"I don't need help."

"You should be resting. You don't look like you got a wink of sleep last night."

"It's hard to sleep when you're carrying around

a beach ball in your middle," she said dryly. "But I'm used to it, so don't worry about me."

Her fragile strength struck him again. He was impressed and frustrated all in one shot.

"What can I do to help?" he repeated.

Her mouth tightened. "Leave town?" she suggested with a sweetness that didn't fool him.

The hall was silent. A clock somewhere in the lower reaches of the old house ticked loudly into the thick stillness.

"I'm sorry." She pressed her fingers to her eyes, closed them briefly. "I don't want to sound rude," she said then, dropping her hands. "You're right, I'm tired. But that's not why you're offering to help me. You have ulterior motives. And I'm too tired to deal with them right now, okay? The best way you can help me, honestly, would be to leave me alone. Please."

Garrett stared at her. She was right, he had ulterior motives. And he wasn't quite sure of what those motives were anymore. He wanted to get her to agree to the testing, but was that all he wanted?

He didn't know the answer to his own question, though he could see how much his presence was adding to her stress and pressure. That fact hit him hard suddenly, and he felt like a coldhearted jerk.

But hadn't he come to Deer Creek specifically to pressure Lanie? Why was he feeling guilty now for doing exactly what he'd come to do?

"I promise I'll leave after breakfast." He compromised with himself as well as her. "But only if you let me help you."

She sighed. "All right. But honestly, right now, all I'm going to do is get the dough started for the cinnamon rolls. If you want to come down in a couple hours, you can help me get set up then."

He smiled. "Good."

"I still have Ben's things," she said when he started to turn away.

Garrett stared at her.

"His clothes," she explained. "I can get you a T-shirt, some shorts, so you have something to, uh, wear. I'll just leave them outside your door."

And that was when he realized he was standing there in her hall, having a conversation, in nothing but his briefs. It occurred to him that she didn't look at all embarrassed. He was sure for a second that she actually looked…interested.

Then she turned around and walked away, and he wasn't sure of anything at all.

Lanie punched the soft dough, turning the large bowl, punching again. And again. Harder. Working out the tight knots of frustration that clenched her muscles at the same time that she created the bread.

He was going to leave. So why was she still frustrated?

Because he still believed she was some kind of con artist? Or because of the way he'd made her feel in the hall when he'd stared at her with his dark, hard eyes? He'd noticed her. And she'd noticed him—his bare chest, strong legs, broad shoulders.

The way he'd stared at her hadn't meant anything, she reminded herself. She'd probably imagined it. She looked like the side of a barn, and he was a handsome, virile man. Was she actually imagining for one single second that he could have been attracted to her?

She almost laughed, but a weird little lump in her throat turned it into a hard gulp. She recognized the bane of her pregnancy—hormones. Sniffling, blinking several times rapidly, she turned the dough for cinnamon rolls into a greased dish and covered it with a damp towel. She washed her hands, dried them, then went back upstairs, climbing the stairs with little energy.

She was just tired. Really tired. And a little bit scared. She hadn't told Garrett the whole truth.

She'd been having contractions all night, erratic but sharp.

There was nothing to be done, no reason to panic, she kept telling herself. The contractions were irregular and widely spaced. The doctor had told her not to go to the hospital until the pains were much closer together. First-time moms were notorious for long labors, according to all the pregnancy guidebooks. So even if she did turn out to be in labor for real, she had time. She would get through the morning by sheer willpower. She would see the Berringers—and Garrett—off. Then she would get to the hospital, even if she had to call someone to help her—one of her friends or an ambulance.

The most magical thing that had ever happened to her was discovering she was pregnant after Ben's death. She wasn't going to let the Blakemores' distrust and accusations spoil the joy of this day.

She didn't want Garrett standing outside her hospital door, demanding tests.

His question from the night before came back to her. *Why did you marry him?* Was there any chance some small part of him had believed her answer?

He'd agreed to leave this morning and hadn't said a word about the testing—that had surprised her. So had the softness in his eyes, his voice. She'd thought, for just a second, that he really cared.

It had felt nice. For just a second.

And that was exactly why she had to get him out of her house, out of Deer Creek, before she had this baby. She was afraid, terribly afraid, that his softness was a trick, a way to break through her defenses, take over her life—and her baby—before she knew what was happening.

She couldn't afford to take that risk, let him under her skin.

Another contraction hit her in the shower. She squeezed her eyes tight and practiced the breathing exercises she'd learned in birthing class until the wave of pain passed. She dressed and packed a small bag of toiletries for the hospital, which she tucked in the corner of her room.

She dug out a T-shirt, shorts and shoes for Garrett from the boxes of Ben's things she had in the attic. Garrett looked close enough to Ben's size that she was sure they would fit. She left them on the floor outside his door.

Bright morning sunshine filtered through the lace curtains at the windows by the time she headed back downstairs. Her back ached unrelentingly. She wondered how she was going to manage if a contraction hit her in front of Garrett. Maybe she'd been so rude and unwelcoming, he would change his mind about helping her. Maybe he would just leave.

No such luck, she realized when he arrived in the kitchen right on schedule. The T-shirt stretched over his chest and shoulders, revealing every muscle. He looked so…different. Casual. Not the uptight businessman at all.

She stared at him, feeling weirdly as if she were seeing someone else entirely. Her whole image of Garrett Blakemore shifted and transformed. He looked human, approachable. Sexy.

"Good morning," he said.

The crisp, clean smell of him nearly took over her senses. She backed up a few steps, away from his evocative maleness.

"Hi." Ripping her gaze from him, she focused on her work. "Here, you can cut these up while I cook the eggs." She pushed a cutting board, knife and a pile of apples and bananas down the counter toward him.

The sooner they got breakfast ready, the sooner he'd leave.

"All right." He moved to the counter obediently and got down to work.

She slid the prepared cinnamon rolls into the preheated oven and started cracking eggs over a skillet on the stove. For several minutes the kitchen was quiet but for the strike of the knife on the cutting board and the sizzle of the eggs cooking in the pan.

Garrett glanced at Lanie, her back so stiff and straight. Her body language was unfriendly, to say the least.

"That was interesting, what you were telling the Berringers about how long this house has been in your family," he said casually.

"My great-grandparents built it," she said, pouring milk into the pan. She didn't look back at him.

"Did you grow up in Deer Creek?" he asked.

"Mostly. I was born in Tyler. My parents died when I was two, and after that my baby brother and I came to live here with my grandmother."

"Does your brother live around here?"

"He's in the military, stationed in Germany, so I don't see him often."

"You must miss your grandmother."

She didn't say anything.

Garrett cored another apple. "We have something in common. I lost my parents to an airline accident when I was nine."

Lanie turned finally and met his eyes. "I'm sorry. Ben told me about it."

And despite all her obvious wariness, he could see a shimmer of compassion in her eyes.

It would be easy to sink into those deep blue pools of sympathy. He hardened himself against the urge to fall—and fall hard.

"It's not going to be easy, raising a baby on your own," he said, deliberately bringing the conversation around to the whole point of his being in Deer Creek and standing in her kitchen.

Her eyes shuttered immediately. She turned back to the pan, stirring the eggs.

"I'll manage," she said coolly.

She didn't want to talk about the baby, that was clear. Garrett narrowed his eyes, watching her. The sleeveless dress she wore bared her shoulders, the skin pale and soft looking. Her long hair was pulled back in a tight ponytail, but pale, wavy tendrils had broken loose to feather her cheeks.

"Is the baby a boy or a girl?" he asked. "You haven't said."

"I don't know," she answered. "I didn't want them to tell me."

"What are you hoping for?" he probed.

She pivoted. "Do you really care what I'm hoping for?" she demanded suddenly. "Do you really care what I think or feel—about anything?" After giving him about two seconds to respond, she continued, "I didn't think so." She reached into a cabinet and took down a bowl. "Would you mind setting the fruit out on the sideboard?"

"Hey, wait a minute. I never said I didn't care."
What *was* he saying?

"So you do care? You care about the feelings of a gold-digging con artist?" Her eyes flashed. The light skin of her cheeks suffused with color. "Isn't that how you think of me?"

A beat passed. "I don't know," Garrett admitted, unaccustomed confusion swirling inside him. "If you'd have the testing done—"

"Ah, the testing. I knew we'd come back to that. Let's cut the chitchat and go straight there." She turned the heat off on the stove, moved the pan of cooked eggs back to a cool burner and crossed her arms.

"Is it so unreasonable for Walter to expect proof that this baby is his heir?"

"Is it so impossible for you to accept that I don't care?" she returned simply.

He looked into her eyes and saw nothing but sincerity there. Uncertainty filled him. He wanted to believe her, wished desperately he could trust the artlessness of those blue depths.

But it wasn't that easy.

Lanie turned away then, her shoulders stiffer than ever. He watched her scrape the eggs into a polished silver warming tray. He wanted to say something, anything, but he couldn't. He wasn't even sure what it was that he wanted to say.

She took the cinnamon rolls out of the oven, and he helped her carry everything into the dining room and set up. Silence swelled between them as they worked.

The Berringers arrived downstairs. After giving a cheerful greeting, Lanie retreated to the kitchen. Garrett didn't feel particularly welcome to follow her, so he poured himself a cup of coffee and tried one of her fresh, hot cinnamon rolls. It was delicious. He watched Mrs. Berringer inhale three rolls along with a mountain of eggs, while he listened to Mr. Berringer detail the couple's itinerary for the day.

When the Berringers finished eating and went upstairs to collect their things, Garrett carried an armload of dishes into the kitchen. Lanie was sponging off the counter. She turned on the faucet over the sink and started washing dishes when he set the plates and cups on the counter.

"Thank you for helping with breakfast." She didn't look up.

"Aren't you going to eat?" he asked.

"I'm not hungry."

He stood there for another minute, watching her wash dishes.

"All right." He reached in the back pocket of his shorts, took out his wallet and withdrew his business card. He set it on the counter near Lanie. "Here's the number to my office in Austin."

"I won't need it."

"I'd like to know when the baby's born," he said. He couldn't force her to go back to Austin with him. He'd decided it was time to pick his battles. The testing was more important than getting her to Austin. "We'll talk then."

Upstairs in his room, he got his things together. He was stepping back into the hall when Mrs. Berringer's huge form appeared at the top of the stairwell. She was huffing and flushed.

"Mr. Blakemore!" She paused, her ample chest heaving as she fought to catch her breath. "Come quickly. You've got to get your wife to the hospital right this minute!"

Chapter Five

Garrett pushed past Mrs. Berringer and barreled down the stairs. Lanie was sitting on the couch in the parlor. Mr. Berringer perched beside her, patting her hand. The couple's suitcases were by the door.

"Are you all right?" Garrett demanded, his pulse racing.

"I'm fine," Lanie said. "I just had another contraction, that's all."

She looked guilty, and he suspected she hadn't been honest with him earlier about thinking she was in false labor.

Horror streaked through him. What if he and the Berringers had left and she'd been somehow unable to get to the hospital by herself? What would have happened to her and the baby?

He felt competely shaken by the thought.

"That wasn't just any contraction," Mrs. Berringer announced, lumbering up behind him. "It lasted a full minute. That baby's on the way."

Mr. Berringer helped Lanie rise.

"Where's your hospital bag, honey?" Mrs. Berringer asked.

Lanie told her, and by the time Garrett brought it back down to the parlor, the Berringers were stowing their own suitcases in their car, and Lanie was waiting for him by the door.

The spring morning shone crisp and bright.

Mrs. Berringer came back to Lanie. "Everything is going to be all right, honey," she said. "After the baby is born, you won't even remember the pain, I promise. It'll be all joy."

"Thank you," Lanie said. "I hope you're right!" As soon as the Berringers left, she turned to Garrett. "You don't really have to drive me to the hospital. There's no need for you to change your plans. I can manage just fine on my own."

Garrett expelled an exasperated breath. Why did he always feel like he was knocking his head against a brick wall with her? He picked up her bag from where she'd set it by the door.

"I'm not leaving you to manage on your own," he said grimly. "I'm driving you to the hospital. Now if you really want to do something, you can tell me what you were thinking when you lied to me this morning about being in labor."

He stalked off with her bag, leaving Lanie no choice but to follow, unless she wanted to physically wrest her bag from him, and under the circumstances she didn't quite feel up to that.

She tagged after him, anger bubbling up, adding to the already churning mix of anxiety and panic inside her. "I didn't lie to you," she argued. "I just didn't tell you the whole truth."

"Oh, that's different." He held open the passenger door.

She sat. He slammed the door and walked around to his side. The car revved loudly to life, and they sped off down the street. The luxury vehicle with its perfect shocks took the road like velvet, and it was incredibly quiet inside, nothing but the purr of expensive machinery.

"It wasn't any of your business," Lanie answered him after a minute.

"What were you planning to do?" he demanded harshly, turning onto the main street through the town square. He cast her a brief, harsh glance. "Why didn't you tell me you might be in real labor?"

"I was going to drive myself to the hospital. Barring that, I could have called 911."

"And what were you doing cooking breakfast while you were in labor, anyway?" he asked, cutting her another hard glance.

"My pregnancy book says to carry on with your usual activities during early labor, that it's the best way to keep your mind off things. It's—oh, never mind. Why am I explaining this to you?" She stared determinedly out the window.

"Why were you trying so hard to get rid of me before you had the baby?"

"Why wouldn't I want to get rid of you?" she asked rhetorically. "You're overbearing and insulting." Scenery whipped by. "I don't need your help, and I don't want your help."

"Are you hiding something?"

"Of course, that's it. My secret lover, the true father of the baby, is going to meet me at the hospital. You've caught me," she deadpanned, turning to glare at him. "Now my plan to bilk Walter will never work."

Garrett slammed on the brakes and pulled to a stop at the side of the road.

Lanie gripped the door handle with one hand for support from the near neck-snapping stop. "What? What's the matter?"

"I have absolutely no idea where the hospital is. Am I going in the right direction?" Garrett combed his fingers roughly through his thick, dark hair, his expression frazzled.

Lanie realized both of them had been so busy arguing, they'd lost sight of what they were doing. She'd even forgotten the unending pain in her back for a few minutes, which was the only good thing about their otherwise horrible conversation.

The sensation smashed back into her, along with a wash of emotion. She wasn't up to this skirmish. She was about to have her baby, and this wasn't the atmosphere into which she wanted her child to be born. Also, she couldn't afford to use up all her energy this way. She needed her strength for what lay ahead, the birth.

"This is exactly why I was trying to get rid of you," she said, her voice taut. "This is supposed to be one of the best days of my life. Probably *the* best day of my life. I'm alone. My best friend—my labor coach—is out of town. I have no parents, no husband. Just my husband's family, who all think I'm—I'm—" She reached for the worst thing she could think of in her mixed-up, emotional state, "—the Wicked Witch of the West." She was absolutely not going to cry.

A tear welled up, slipped out. She closed her eyes, turned her head away from him.

The car was so still and silent. She fought the urge to break into weak sobs.

A soft touch brushed her chin. His warm fingers drew her around to face him, sliding gently up her cheek to rub the fat tear away. She opened her eyes and found his intense dark gaze on hers.

"I don't think you're the Wicked Witch of the West," he said, his voice hushed but clearly audible to her in the confines of the car. "If you were, you couldn't cry. It would make you melt."

And she stared at him for a really long moment before another tear fell at the same time that she laughed.

"That was so dumb," she said shakily. "I can't believe you said that." And she couldn't. It had been too silly. It wasn't something she would have imagined Garrett Blakemore saying.

"It made you laugh, didn't it?" he said, dropping his hand from her cheek. "Look, I'm—I'm sorry." The words seemed to come from him with difficulty. "You just scared the daylights out of me, that's all."

Lanie's breath caught. She studied his face, conflicted by what she saw. Underneath his brusque exterior lurked a soft heart, she was absolutely positive of it now. He was domineering and cold when he wanted to be, but that wasn't all there was to him. He had this amazingly sweet, funny, caring side. The knowledge was unsettling.

"Could we call a truce?" he asked. "At least long enough for me to get you to the hospital?"

Lanie swallowed thickly. "Okay."

She gave him directions to the hospital, and Garrett put the car back into gear and hit the road. Nothing was more than a five-minute drive in Deer Creek, and once they were headed the right way they arrived at their destination in no time.

Another contraction rolled over her as they parked. She felt limp when it was over, and ridiculously grateful for Garrett's strong arm to lean on when she was finally ready to walk inside the building.

It was easy, way too easy, to lean on Garrett when he wasn't being arrogant and bossy.

An elderly woman in a pink jacket greeted Lanie by name as they walked in the front door of Deer Creek Community Medical Center. It was a small but up-to-date facility, and Lanie knew many of the retiree volunteers as friends of her grandmother's.

Mrs. Poston was plump, with tight white curls. Her friendly smile was a cheering sight. She noted the small overnight case Garrett had insisted on carrying inside for Lanie.

"Are you here to have your baby, dear?" she questioned eagerly.

"I think so," Lanie told her, a glow of warmth shooting through her as she and Garrett walked to the bank of elevators across the lobby. It hit her, really hard, that this was the day she would finally hold her baby. And it was difficult to maintain bad feelings toward anyone—even Garrett Blakemore.

The elevator arrived and they stepped inside. She pushed the button for the second floor and watched Garrett from the corner of her eye.

She had no idea what had shaped him into the man he was today, but she suspected it couldn't have been easy for a grieving boy to have been placed under the austere guardianship of a man like Walter Blakemore. Garrett couldn't have been shown much love and warmth. She knew Ben hadn't felt loved, and Ben had been Walter Blakemore's own son.

She knew Garrett had been through a divorce, too. Had his marriage contributed to his shell of hardness and distrust?

"Thanks for bringing me to the hospital," she said softly as the elevator opened onto the maternity wing. "So you'll be going back to Austin now."

He shook his head. "I'll hang around."

It was on the tip of her tongue to automatically argue with this statement, but she didn't. Something held her back.

"I'd better get checked in," she said.

She was preregistered, so the sign-in process was efficient, and in minutes she was escorted to a private birthing room.

Garrett stood there for several minutes, not sure what to do, where to go. He had no intention of leaving the building. If she was having Ben's baby, then he had an obligation to his family to be on hand for the child's birth.

At least, that was the only coherent reason he had for hanging around.

He wandered around and wound up standing in front of a glass window into the hospital nursery. Two babies slept, swaddled in soft-looking receiving blankets. Another infant squawked in protest as a nurse bathed him. An unbelievable blossom of tenderness expanded automatically inside Garrett's chest. Tenderness—and awe. He couldn't recall the last time he'd seen a newborn child. He couldn't imagine holding one. They looked so utterly fragile and precious.

He stared at them for a long time. He'd sworn off marriage, and that meant there would be no babies in his future. He'd been fine, just fine, with that decision. But when he turned away from the nursery window, he was unsettled.

The waiting room was empty. There was a rack

stuffed with magazines, and a television against the far wall. He walked to the large window. The medical center was on the edge of town, and this angle yielded a pleasant vista of the rolling, wooded hills for which the area got its name.

He stood there for a long time, staring out at the peaceful rural landscape. He thought about turning on the television, or reading a magazine, but he felt too restless. After a while he checked at the nurses' station.

"Mrs. Blakemore hasn't delivered yet" was all he could get out of them.

He started pacing.

"Mrs. Blakemore? How are you doing?"

"Bored," Lanie managed around the thermometer the nurse stuck in her mouth. The thermometer beeped and the nurse removed it. "What do you think? Soon?" she asked hopefully.

"Hmm." The nurse consulted the paper readout from the machine that monitored Lanie's contractions. It was hooked up to Lanie by a belt across her stomach. "That's hard to say. Looks like your contractions are starting to speed up, though. Might not be too long."

Lanie grinned happily. "Good." Since she'd had a regional nerve block—an epidural—she'd been relieved of the agonizing pain.

"So tell me. Who's the gorgeous man out there asking about you every five minutes?" the nurse asked as she checked Lanie's blood pressure.

"Does he really ask about me every five minutes?" Lanie asked, feeling a silly little urge to smile that made no sense at all. She should be wishing Garrett Blakemore would get in his car and drive back to Austin. Why was she flattered to hear he was worrying outside her door?

Because he was really a sweet guy under all that gruffness. Or was she kidding herself?

How would she ever know unless she gave him another chance?

The nurse laughed. "Well, not quite every five minutes. But almost. Would you like him to come in to keep you company for a little while? He sure keeps looking over here as if he'd like to."

Lanie wondered if she'd lost her mind. She'd gone soft, that was for sure, because she heard herself saying, "Yes, please ask him to come in."

It was a day for new beginnings, and it might be the stupidest thing she'd ever done, but she was going to give Garrett one more chance.

Chapter Six

Garrett knocked on the door to Lanie's room. "Hello?" he called softly. He pushed the door open, poked his head inside the room. "The nurse said it was okay for me to come in."

Lanie nodded. "Uh-huh. Come in." She was propped up in the bed, wearing a thin blue hospital gown that was hiked up to accommodate some sort of contraption wrapped over her middle. It was connected to a machine on the floor beside her. A sheet covered her lower body.

"How are you doing?" he asked awkwardly. He hadn't realized how intimate and personal it would feel to be here in her hospital room. He didn't belong—yet he was inexplicably drawn to be there.

"Bored." She stared at him pointedly. "Obviously I'm desperate for company." The glimmer of laughter in her voice and the quirk of her mouth kept the jab from sounding harsh.

"Obviously," Garrett bounced back. She was looking at him as if he were a human being instead of an ogre—for a change. He liked it. He liked it a lot. "What's that?" He nodded at the machine.

"That's an external fetal monitor," she explained. She touched the belt around her stomach. "It shows when I'm having contractions. See, I'm having one right now." She indicated the readout.

Garrett stared at her, then at the monitor, then back at her. "Why don't you look like you're in pain?"

She laughed. "I had an epidural a couple hours ago, right after I got here. It's a nerve block."

Garrett couldn't take his gaze off her, transfixed by the glow in her eyes. "I see," he said. He didn't, of course. He had no idea what she was talking about, but evidently she was no longer in pain and he was happy about that.

He struggled for conversation. Now that he was here, he didn't know what he was supposed to say, how to act. He'd never been inside a laboring woman's hospital room before.

"Are you hungry? Do you want me to ask them to bring you some lunch?" He realized it was nearly noon. He was a little hungry himself.

She shook her head. "I'd love to eat, but I can't. All I can have is ice. You can go to the cafeteria if you want."

Garrett couldn't imagine going off to lunch

knowing she was hungry and not allowed to eat. "I'm not hungry," he lied.

"You can sit down, you know."

Lanie was very aware of Garrett's gaze on her as he sat in the armchair near the bed. She could hear the muted sound of a baby crying somewhere down the hall.

"This is a nice little hospital," Garrett commented casually.

Lanie reached for her cup of ice chips, tipped it up to her lips.

She munched and swallowed the ice before answering. "Deer Creek is a nice little town. It's a wonderful, safe place to raise a child." She had a sinking feeling Walter's next command could be that she raise his grandchild in the city. She wondered if she could head that potential problem off at the pass by convincing Garrett of Deer Creek's charms.

A twinge of discomfort rippled over her middle then, distracting her. Was the epidural wearing off? She wondered if the nurse would be back to check on her again soon.

"Do you have names picked out?" Garrett asked.

"Anne Marie if it's a girl. Anne for my grandmother, Marie for my mother."

"Those are beautiful names," he commented. "What if it's a boy?"

"Dalton. Dalton Benjamin." She felt instantly defensive. She didn't want to remember he didn't trust this baby was truly Ben's—but she couldn't forget it. "Dalton was my father's name. And Benjamin, of course…"

He said nothing for a moment. "It must be painful for you that Ben isn't here today." His face stiffened into strained lines.

"I wish he could have been here," she said. "I'm sorry that my baby won't ever know its father."

She watched Garrett get up, pace to the draped window, his hands jammed in the pockets of the shorts. She remembered how close he and Ben had been as children. For the first time it struck her that he had to be grieving for Ben. And she was ashamed that she hadn't even considered it before.

Impulsively she decided to tell Garrett the truth—because he deserved the truth. And because maybe, just maybe, he would believe her.

"Ben and I never discussed having children," she said quietly.

Garrett turned, his features shadowed, the muted morning sunlight glowing through the draped window behind him.

"You hadn't?" he asked.

"No." She swallowed, forced herself to continue. "I don't think our marriage was going to make it." The hospital noises outside her door seemed to recede. All she could see was his shadowed face, all she could hear was the long breath he expelled before he spoke.

"You said you loved him."

"I did."

It seemed to take several seconds for understanding to dawn. He took two steps toward her, his face coming into the light of the lamp by her bed, his expression grim. "You're saying it was Ben who wasn't happy? Ben gave up everything for you."

"It wasn't me that Ben wanted so desperately. He wanted to break away from his father, which was a backward way of trying to get Walter's attention—to make Walter see him, love him, for who he was, not for what Walter wanted him to be."

Garrett didn't know what was harder to believe—that Ben had wanted to break away from Walter so badly that he would deliberately go into an ill-fated marriage, or that Ben could have lived with this beautiful woman and not been happy.

"And you married him, anyway?" he asked roughly. How could he not have realized that Ben had become that desperate? Had he been so absorbed in his own troubles with Vanessa that he had let Ben down so badly? Guilt slashed through him.

"I didn't know. I didn't realize the depth of the emotional power struggle he was involved in with his father." She shook her head. "Walter wanted him in the company, and Ben didn't want to be part of it. He thought if he married me, he could force his father to accept that—to accept him. But Walter cut him off instead. And Ben was too proud, too angry, too hurt, to approach his father then."

Garrett stared at her. If what she was saying was

true, she was the one conned, not Ben. She was the one used.

He'd known Ben had had trouble settling into the family business. He'd been young, restless. It had been difficult for Garrett to understand. Without Walter, Garrett would have been in a foster home. He owed everything to his uncle, had followed in his footsteps out of instinctive duty.

"I'm not blaming Ben," she went on almost as if she could read his thoughts. "He was hurting too much to realize he was hurting me, too."

"Why are you telling me this?" he demanded, eyeing her suspiciously. Every iota of the tension between them was back, and some visceral part of him hated that.

She flinched at his harsh tone, but she held her head high. "Because it's the truth."

Frustration clawed at Garrett's gut, making him feel ill. He was tired of doubts and mistrust. But he felt like he was in a deep hole of suspicion. Every time he tried to climb out, he slipped right back down.

"Because it's why I wrote that letter to Walter," she said. "I wanted for my baby what Ben had wanted for himself, but never got," she said. "Walter's love. It was naive of me, I suppose, but I thought Ben's death might have changed Walter. Obviously it hasn't. He sent you here with a whole list of demands. He wants to test the baby so he can name him or her as his *heir,* so he can give him everything that destroyed Ben. He still can't give the one thing that matters—love.''

Garrett could only listen in stunned silence, staring at her. Was this some sort of clever manipulation? He didn't know what to think. Everything he'd thought about Ben's last months was turned upside down.

''I'm scared of what more he'll want if I give him the tests,'' she went on, her voice shaking with sudden emotion. ''Will he demand we move to Austin, where he can dictate every move we—oh!'' She broke off, her features painfully contorted.

Garrett ate up the space between them with quick strides, responding automatically to her pain. ''What is it? I thought you weren't supposed to feel the contractions.''

''The epidural…is…wearing off,'' she whispered tightly. She huffed air in and out. ''Definitely. I can feel this contraction.''

''What do I do? Do you want me to get the nurse?''

''Yes…please…get the nurse.''

Garrett ran to the door. The hall was empty. He sped to the nurses' station. The nurse that had been in Lanie's room before wasn't there, but he found another one and brought her back.

He waited in the hall while the nurse checked Lanie. Stress worked at his nerves. He needed this baby to be born so he could get out of this town, away from Lanie. Get where he could think straight.

When he looked in her beautiful blue eyes, he couldn't think at all.

The nurse emerged. Through the open door he saw Lanie lying on her side in the bed, her back to him.

"Is she all right?" he asked the nurse.

"It won't be long now," she said briskly.

He heard Lanie take a sharp breath. "She's having another contraction already," he said, stunned.

The nurse nodded. "They're going to keep getting closer. She's not going to get much break now. She's progressing fast now, real fast—she's almost fully dilated. You can rub her back if that helps her. Keep reminding her to breathe in and out. We don't want her hyperventilating. Try to get her to relax between contractions. I'm going to get the doctor."

Garrett blinked, but before he could say anything, the nurse hurried off.

"Lanie?" He walked up to the bed cautiously. Obviously the nurse thought he was Lanie's husband. He wasn't, but that didn't mean he could leave Lanie alone, no matter how confused he was about the things she'd said. He reached the bed. The hospital gown, tied at the back of her neck, gaped open to reveal the creamy column of her spine. Gingerly he placed his hands inside the gown, massaged her shoulders and neck like the nurse had told him.

He worked to apply counterpressure to her pain. Her skin was warm, pliant. She moaned.

"Breathe," he murmured. "You're doing well."

She turned as the contraction passed, stared straight at him, anxiety shining in her eyes. "I don't think they're going to give me any more of the epidural. She said it's too late, there's no time. The baby's coming." She drew in a shaky breath. "I'm having the baby, now, without any medication. Oh, no," she whispered raspily. "I'm having another contraction."

"It's only been a minute since the last one," Garrett said. She was already desperately hissing air in and out.

He didn't know what to do. She was turned around now, so he couldn't rub her back anymore. He put his hand over hers instead. She gripped it back with surprising ferocity and wouldn't let go.

"You're doing just fine," he said as the contraction receded, struggling for the right thing to say or do. "Try to relax now."

"How am I supposed to relax?" she snapped at him.

"I don't know! The nurse told me to say that." He stared at her, taking in the fatigue and fear in her eyes. "Do you want me to go now?" he asked, torn between wanting to stay and feeling uncharacteristically weak in the knees at the idea of witnessing a birth. "I'll leave you alone."

Lanie chewed her lip, stared at Garrett. She should tell him to go. He wasn't her husband. He wasn't even her friend. But no matter how many books she'd read and how many classes she'd attended, childbirth was a formidable mystery.

Garrett's hand felt so big and warm and *secure*. The idea of letting go of it suddenly terrified her.

"Could you just—just hold my hand?" she asked with a quaver she couldn't quite control.

Garrett knew then he couldn't leave her. For once, Lanie actually *wanted* his help, wasn't pushing him away. Another contraction hit. She squeezed his hand so hard he could feel her nails biting into his flesh.

The nurse ran into the room pushing a cart of instruments. She flipped over an extension at the end of the bed, pulled a huge light down from the ceiling and flashed it on before ripping the sheet off Lanie's lower body. Garrett whipped around, facing the head of the bed, out of automatic respect for her modesty—not to mention his jellied knees.

"I feel pressure," Lanie cried.

"Don't push," the nurse ordered. "You can't push yet. Blow."

Lanie blew out, then let her head fall back as the contraction slipped away. Sweat beaded her forehead, dampening the tendrils of hair escaping her ponytail.

The doctor burst into the room and Garrett swerved his head around, carefully maintaining his level of sight above the bed. The doctor wore surgical garments and gloves. He went straight to the end of Lanie's bed.

"She's fully dilated," the nurse said.

"How's it going, Lanie?" Dr. Furley said cheerfully. He was an older man, and his confident buoyance relieved some of Garrett's anxiety.

"It's time, dear," the nurse said. "Next contraction, you can push. I can see the hair on his little head—and this baby's got plenty, let me tell you."

"Really?" Lanie whispered.

Garrett looked back at her. Her eyes were huge and elated for a minute, and she seemed to gain a second wind. Then another contraction hit.

"Sit up, dear," the nurse ordered. "Sit up."

Garrett helped her, supporting her back with one hand, his other hand still in hers.

Lanie squeezed her eyes shut and pushed. Several contractions and pushes later, Garrett's hand was nearly numb from her death grip, but he worried about Lanie, who was pale and trembling. At the same time, he was awed by her courage and self-possession. He knew she was scared, knew she was in pain, but she hadn't fallen apart. She just kept going. And he was incredibly proud and honored to have any small part in helping her.

"Okay, okay, next time," the doctor encouraged her. "You're close."

Garrett helped her into position as another contraction came. She gritted her teeth and put all her might into the effort. She was so focused, he wasn't sure she even knew he was there anymore. Then she looked up at him. Pain and exhaustion radiated from her eyes.

"Come on," he urged. "You can do it."

"The baby's coming," the nurse cried. "Push!"

Lanie bore down again. Garrett turned his head in time to see the doctor lift the tiny, wet, red-skinned baby into the air.

Chapter Seven

"It's a boy," Garrett announced into the receiver of the pay phone in the hospital lobby. His heart still sang in reverent wonder. He felt exhilarated. And moved. Moved like he'd never been moved by anything before in his whole life.

"A boy." Walter sounded satisfied. "Good. He's healthy?"

"He's absolutely perfect." Garrett remembered how the baby had bawled as he'd been placed on Lanie's stomach, how Lanie had reached down with gentle awe to touch him for the first time. How she'd looked up at him—Garrett—and smiled through her tears.

And how very close he'd felt to her in that magic instant.

"What did she name him?" Walter asked, his gruff voice breaking into Garrett's thoughts.

"Dalton. Dalton *Benjamin Blakemore*." It wasn't until after Garrett said the baby's name the second time, the full name, that he realized the subconscious emphasis he'd put on the middle and surname. Was there a part of him, a very large part of him, that simply believed this baby was Ben's because Lanie said so?

He hadn't had a chance yet to digest everything Lanie had told him about Ben just before the baby's birth. But it was getting harder and harder for him to think of her as a scheming con artist.

"Have you talked to her about the testing?" Walter demanded.

"She refused to have the baby tested."

"She can't refuse."

"She's the mother," Garrett pointed out.

"And that boy might be my grandson." Walter was silent a long moment. "She must have expenses at a time like this. Hospital bills. Offer her a check. Up front. Just for having the boy tested. The money is hers, even if he's not Ben's."

The old man's voice hardened. "I have to know the truth, Garrett. I have to know if that baby boy is my grandson."

"Hello." Garrett's face appeared around the half-open door to Lanie's hospital room. "Am I interrupting?"

Lanie shook her head. "Come in." She pushed the movable tray away from her bed. "I'm finished eating." The hospital had brought her an early dinner, and she felt one hundred times better now that she'd eaten.

She also felt better for having showered. She was wearing her own gown and robe that she'd brought with her from home. Now that everything was over, she was a little embarrassed. But she couldn't forget how Garrett had held her hand, how he'd encouraged her and supported her and helped her focus.

It was an intimacy that was premature, though, and now that the crisis was passed, she felt awkward.

Her face heated as she watched him come into the room. He walked first to the portable crib and stared down at Dalton, and she wondered if Garrett felt a little uncomfortable, too.

The baby had been bathed and swaddled, and after nursing briefly, he'd gone to sleep. She saw Garrett's granite features soften as he stared downward.

Her pulse fluttered when he shifted his enigmatic gaze to her.

"He looks like you," he said.

"He looks like my brother Hayden to me. And Hayden looks like my dad. I really look a lot more like my mother. I think Dalton is a throwback."

She barely restrained adding the caveat that Dalton had Ben's dark hair. She wasn't sure why she didn't say it, except that she knew it would bring back all that horrible tension between them, and she couldn't help not wanting that.

"How are you feeling?" he asked.

"Good," she said. "Relieved that it's over."

"Me, too," he said with a knowing grin that had Lanie's cheeks flushing again. He came around the bed and sat down in the chair. "You look embarrassed."

"I'm humiliated," Lanie admitted. "Did I hurt your hand?"

"That sounds like one of those questions women ask that can be a trap," he said, his lips quirking upward. "After what I just saw you go through, I'm not going to say you hurt my hand."

"Smart move."

"You don't need to be embarrassed, though," Garrett said.

She stared at him.

"Your modesty was not compromised, if that's what you're worried about," he said gently. "My knees were feeling like Jell-O in there. I didn't have the guts to look."

She laughed. "Okay, thanks." She brushed over his comments, still embarrassed. "Thanks for being there, for holding my hand. All these months, I've been counting on Patty being there with me. I thought I was ready—I read all the books and took all the classes. I did everything you're supposed to do. But when it was time for the real thing, I panicked."

"You didn't look like you were panicking. You did great."

His praise warmed her. She started to feel more at ease.

Dalton squinched up his face and let out a lusty squeal.

"Will you get him for me?" She hated to move her sore, stiff body. And she didn't really want Garrett to see her present ungainly shuffle. She'd been embarrassed enough in front of the man for one day.

Garrett blinked. "All right." He got up and went back to the crib.

Lanie had a hunch he'd never held a newborn baby before. "He won't break," she promised. "Just put one hand on the back of his head, support his neck, and the rest is easy."

Garrett reached down, scooped the infant gingerly into his arms. Dalton was so tiny, and Garrett so big. Lanie's breath caught as she watched him lift the baby to his chest. Dalton's cries turned to little mewls as Garrett drew him closer. The glow of wonder in Garrett's eyes touched her, deep inside.

"He's so light," he breathed. "It's almost like holding air."

"Isn't he beautiful?" she couldn't resist saying. "I can hardly stop staring at him for a minute. I think I'm going to take him home and just stare at him for at least a week."

Garrett tenderly placed Dalton into her arms, then sat again. She snuggled the baby in her arms, smiling down at him. Dalton quieted, gazed back at her with sleepy, liquid-blue eyes. She felt such a well of peace and warmth inside, and it extended to Garrett, she realized. He was part of what had happened today.

She looked up and caught him watching her, and in that brief unguarded second, she saw something in his eyes. Something she was afraid to define, but it made her flesh tingle.

It made her feel like a woman.

His expression immediately altered, but she knew she hadn't imagined it. Not this time.

"How long will you be staying in the hospital?" he asked.

"Until tomorrow."

"Will you have someone to take you home?"

"Patty will be back in town tomorrow night," Lanie explained. "I already called her and told her about the baby. She's going to come get us."

"Good. What will you be doing about the bed-and-breakfast?"

"I'm going to keep it closed for six weeks, as long as I can afford to."

"I see." Garrett stood, paced a few steps toward the window then came back. "I spoke with Walter. I told him about the baby."

Tension instantly filled her body. "Oh." She didn't want to think about Walter. Not now.

"He sends his best wishes."

She didn't say anything, instinctively holding Dalton closer to her breast. Protectiveness surged inside her, fiercer than she'd ever experienced in her life.

"He wants to help you," he said, staring down at her with his serious eyes.

"How many times do I have to tell you that I don't need help?"

"Walter's lost so much," Garrett went on, his voice low, his gaze steady on hers. "To find he has a grandson now—that means so much to him. He doesn't have anything else."

There was a moment of strained silence.

"That's what I'm afraid of," she told him quietly, finally.

"You don't have to be afraid. It will be different this time, not like it was with Ben."

"What will be different?"

"I'll be there."

"You were there with Ben."

"I didn't understand what was going on. Ben didn't confide in me. I still don't understand what happened. But I promise you, for Ben's sake, I won't let Dalton be hurt—not by anyone."

She stared at him, conflicted and scared. Could she believe him?

Did this mean *he* believed *her?*

"Walter only wants to see to your well-being," he said. "Keeping your business closed can't be easy. And with a new baby, there are doctor bills and other costs. No matter what, you're Ben's widow."

Garrett named a sum that sounded enormous to Lanie's ears.

"And just what is it that Walter expects in return

for this oh-so-generous donation to my well-being?'' she asked tightly.

"The blood and DNA testing, as we discussed. The money is yours to keep, either way.''

Either way. Hurt swamped her, unexpected, deep. Not because Walter didn't trust her. She didn't care what Walter thought. Walter scared her, but he couldn't hurt her. Not really.

Garrett could, though, and that knowledge was both shocking and painful.

"No.'' Emotion clogged her throat, made her feel nauseous.

"Lanie—''

"No! The answer is no. You can take that back to Walter. Now get out of my room. In fact, get out of Deer Creek.'' She bit the inside of her cheek to keep from crying in front of him and pressed the buzzer built into the arm of the bed.

A nurse's voice came over the intercom system. "Can I help you, Mrs. Blakemore?''

Lanie stared at Garrett. "Please leave,'' she said quietly, controlling her voice with effort. "I don't want to cause a scene, but I will. I can get hospital security in here if I have to.''

There was something in his face then that nearly tore her apart. She thought for a second, one insane second, that she had hurt him, too.

And then he walked away.

She burst into tears the instant her door swung shut behind him.

Hormones, she told herself. It was just more awful hormones.

But she was lying to herself and she knew it.

Garrett hit the interstate at full speed, blending into the weekend traffic heading toward the city. Frustration simmered through his veins, along with something unsettling that was gnawing at his gut.

He had an hour's drive to remember over and over the pain clouding Lanie's doe eyes when he'd proffered Walter's deal. She'd made him feel like a heel—again.

But it was over. He'd carried out Walter's mission, done his duty. If Walter wanted to pursue further contact with Lanie, he'd have to put his attorney on the job. Garrett was finished with this entire matter.

He was leaving for Japan first thing Monday morning. He had no more time for Lanie and the strange feelings she inspired.

It hit him then what one of those strange feelings was. Regret.

Chapter Eight

He was back.

Lanie considered slamming the door in Garrett's face, leaving him standing on the front porch alone. He was dressed casually, in jeans and a cotton shirt, but he still managed to look crisp and expensive. And transcendently sexy.

She didn't shut the door in his face—for two reasons. One, she figured he'd just start knocking again and not stop until she opened back up, and two, there was this horrible, traitorous little flutter inside her tummy that made her not want to.

She was glad to see him.

It had been nearly four weeks since the day she'd ordered him from her hospital room, and despite how angry she'd been that day—she was glad to see him now. It was irritating.

"Hello," she managed in a voice tempered to convey the lie that he was as interesting to her as a door-to-door vacuum cleaner salesman.

"Hi." He smiled, showing his exceptionally white teeth.

Had she thoroughly appreciated his beautiful mouth before? He had a smile that warmed his strong features, lit his dark eyes. She was sinfully aware of every disgustingly magnetic inch of him.

Time stretched out between them. She could hear a mother calling for her children from a house down the street.

She steeled herself. "What are you doing here?" she asked him, her tone forcibly bland. It was a Saturday morning in June, and the Texas weather was hot and sultry already. That would explain why she was sweating. Except that she was standing in the coolness of the doorway, shaded by the front porch.

"I was worried," Garrett said, watching her steadily with his seductively intense eyes.

"Why?"

"I got back from an overseas business trip this week and I called you—a couple of times. You never picked up the phone." He took a step toward her, closing the gap between them.

She moved back slightly in reaction, her hand still on the doorjamb. Her heart quickened. "The phone always seems to ring just when I've almost got the baby down for a nap." She shrugged lightly. "I hardly ever pick up the phone lately."

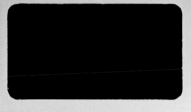

WELCOME TO THE
CASINO!
Try your luck at the Roulette Wheel ...
Play a hand of Twenty-One!

How to play:

1. Play the Roulette and Twenty-One scratch-off games, as instructed on the opposite page, to see that you are eligible for FREE BOOKS and a FREE GIFT!

2. Send back the card and you'll receive TWO brand-new Silhouette Romance® novels. These books have a cover price of $3.50 each in the U.S. and $3.99 each in Canada, but they are yours to keep absolutely free.

3. There's no catch. You're under no obligation to buy anything. We charge nothing — ZERO — for your first shipment. And you don't have to make any minimum number of purchases — not even one!

4. The fact is, thousands of readers enjoy receiving books by mail from the Silhouette Reader Service™ before they're available in stores. They like the convenience of home delivery, and they love our discount prices!

5. We hope that after receiving your free books you'll want to remain a subscriber. But the choice is yours — to continue or cancel, any time at all!

So why not take us up on our invitation, with no risk of any kind. You'll be glad you did!

Play Twenty-One For This Exquisite Free Gift!

THIS SURPRISE
MYSTERY GIFT
WILL BE YOURS
FREE WHEN YOU PLAY
TWENTY-ONE

It's fun, and we're giving away *FREE GIFTS* to all players!

PLAY ROULETTE!

Scratch the silver to see that the ball has landed on 7 RED, making you eligible for TWO FREE romance novels!

PLAY TWENTY-ONE!

Scratch the silver to reveal a winning hand! Congratulations, you have Twenty-One. Return this card promptly and you'll receive a fabulous free mystery gift, along with your free books!

YES!

Please send me all the free Silhouette Romance® books and the gift for which I qualify! I understand that I am under no obligation to purchase any books, as explained on the back of this card.

Name: _____
(PLEASE PRINT)

Address: _____ Apt.#: _____

City: _____ State: _____ Zip: _____

315 SDL CTHG

215 SDL CTG9
(S-R-08/99)

The Silhouette Reader Service™ — Here's how it works:

Accepting your 2 free books and mystery gift places you under no obligation to buy anything. You may keep the books and gift and return the shipping statement marked "cancel." If you do not cancel, about a month later we'll send you 6 additional novels and bill you just $2.90 each in the U.S., or $3.25 each in Canada, plus 25¢ delivery per book and applicable taxes if any.* That's the complete price and — compared to the cover price of $3.50 in the U.S. and $3.99 in Canada — it's quite a bargain! You may cancel at any time, but if you choose to continue, every month we'll send you 6 more books, which you may either purchase at the discount price or return to us and cancel your subscription.

*Terms and prices subject to change without notice. Sales tax applicable in N.Y. Canadian residents will be charged applicable provincial taxes and GST.

If offer card is missing write to: Silhouette Reader Service, 3010 Walden Ave., P.O. Box 1867, Buffalo, NY 14240-9952

BUSINESS REPLY MAIL

FIRST-CLASS MAIL   PERMIT NO 717   BUFFALO NY

POSTAGE WILL BE PAID BY ADDRESSEE

SILHOUETTE READER SERVICE
3010 WALDEN AVE
PO BOX 1867
BUFFALO NY 14240-9952

NO POSTAGE
NECESSARY
IF MAILED
IN THE
UNITED STATES

"I left messages. You didn't call me back."

"We don't have anything to talk about. I'm not interested in Walter's money, or his tests, or anything else." She'd received two letters from Walter's attorney and had ignored them both. She supposed she should have suspected Walter would send Garrett to follow up.

Garrett placed his hand lightly on the door, and she knew he was making sure she couldn't shut it on him.

"How are you?"

She blinked, prepared for arguing and set slightly off-kilter by the way he'd moved right ahead with the conversation as if she hadn't spoken.

"I'm fine."

"And the baby?"

"He's fine."

"Gaining weight?"

"Yes. He weighs ten pounds now." A thread of pride wove into her voice.

"I'd like to see him." Garrett stepped forward, and Lanie had no choice but to get out of the way unless she wanted to physically bar his path. And she wasn't about to do that. Just looking at Garrett did funny, scary things to her insides. She wasn't going to risk making actual contact.

"He's sleeping," she said.

"I'll wait. If you don't mind."

"I'm a little busy," she countered. "This isn't a good time."

"Oh?"

Did he actually look let down, or was she imagining it?

She felt guilty. He was Ben's cousin, and he'd taken the trouble to come. It wasn't right for her to prevent him from seeing Dalton. She wouldn't even prevent Walter from seeing Dalton if he showed up at her house.

"It's just that I'm opening for business again in two weeks, and I'm not ready," she explained weakly. "I decided I'd open the other bedroom, the one that wasn't completely restored. I thought while I had the bed-and-breakfast closed would be a good time to go ahead and finish it up. There's a festival on the square coming up, so it's a chance to have a full house, but—"

"But what?" he prodded.

A cry from upstairs broke between them.

"I need to get him." Lanie turned, fled up the stairs, glad for the chance to get out of the conversation, if only temporarily. She'd been rambling, making excuses, avoiding the truth, which was simply that having him around was more than she could bear.

The last time he'd been around she'd started wanting things she was very afraid he wouldn't—couldn't—give. The man didn't even trust her, he'd made that much patently obvious. How could she even fantasize about having a relationship with a man who didn't trust her? What kind of relationship could they possibly have?

None, she answered herself sternly as she pushed

open the nursery room door. Dalton's cries turned to coos as his bright eyes latched on to her. She walked to the crib, her heart full with the powerful mother's love that energized her every time she looked at her son.

"Hey, sweetheart," she whispered, scooping him into her arms. He nuzzled her and she knew he was hungry. Her nipples tingled in response.

She turned, and almost ran into Garrett.

"Oh," she breathed. "I didn't realize you'd come up here." Her heart pounded. He stood close, so close. He wasn't backing up, and she *couldn't* back up—not without jumping into the crib. With the shades drawn tightly, the room was almost dark despite the sunshiny day. Garrett's eyes glittered in the dim light.

There was a hesitation, mixed with longing, in his gaze. She recognized it all, because she felt the exact same way.

"He's grown so much already," he said, breaking the strange synergy, and looked down at Dalton.

Lanie shifted her attention back to the baby, too, unsettled by what she'd seen in Garrett's eyes.

"Yes, he was at the top of the charts for height and weight at his checkup," she said proudly. "He was small because he was born a few weeks early, but he's making up for it."

"He looks healthy." Garrett reached out, smoothed his hand over the baby's fuzzy head, then tucked a finger against his palm. The baby's hand curled around it, then he turned his small face back toward Lanie.

Dalton's mouth strained, birdlike, at her breasts. She felt herself grow engorged beneath the light-weight T-shirt she wore.

Her cheeks heated almost painfully, and she scooted sideways to get around Garrett. The nursery was at the end of the hall, next to her room. Across the hall was the room she'd been struggling to complete. The door stood open. She'd been working in there, off and on.

She'd been having a moment of optimistic ambition when she'd booked all three guest rooms for the festival weekend. She'd brought in a ladder and cans of paint, and covered the floor with old sheets. After stripping the yellowed wallpaper that had hung there for no telling how many decades, she'd sanded the walls and trim, but that was about as far as she'd gotten.

"You're going to have guests in this room in two weeks? And you're doing all the work?" Garrett looked at her dubiously.

"I can do it." She didn't know how, but she wasn't going to admit that.

Garrett's gaze narrowed, intensified. Light shafted into the hall from the windows of the un-finished guest room. "Are you sure you should be doing this sort of work right after you've had a baby?"

"In some parts of the world, it's customary for women to work in the fields the same day they have babies. Four weeks postpartum, I think I can paint."

He wasn't deterred. "You look tired."

"Of course I'm tired. I have a newborn. It's a law. You can't have a newborn and have a good night's sleep. You can have one or the other, not both."

She shifted Dalton onto her shoulder, patted his back through his little undershirt. Garrett looked worried, and that made her feel like mush inside. She'd had friends bring her gifts and food and all sorts of well wishes and concern—so why was she so affected by Garrett's attention? It was silly and dangerous.

She needed to pull herself together, and as quickly as possible.

"I have to feed Dalton, so please excuse me." She headed for the privacy of her bedroom.

Nursing the baby was a soothing routine, and behind the closed door of her room she managed to slow her heartbeat and her mind enough to examine her confusing reactions. She was tired, as he'd pointed out. Dalton's nighttime sleeping patterns were sporadic at best. Not to mention that Garrett was an attractive, sophisticated man—and she was a small-town girl, flattered by his attention.

But despite her vulnerability, she wasn't naive to the fact that Garrett's attention could be a ploy. He was here because of the baby—not because of her. He didn't even *trust* her.

When Dalton was satisfied, she emerged outside

her room. A swish-swish came to her ears from the new guest room, and she paced quickly to the doorway. Garrett had his back to her, muscles flexing in his arms as he pulled the paint roller down the far wall, spreading the soft peach color in an even stroke.

She stared for several seconds, speechless. "You're painting," she said finally, stupidly. "You don't have to do that. I don't want you to do that."

Garrett drew the roller down and turned. "I just knew you were going to say something like that. That's why I didn't ask."

Lanie was so filled with relief and frustration all at once that she didn't know what to say. She hadn't the slightest idea how she was going to get the room painted in time, between her ever-present exhaustion and the constant interruptions of caring for the baby. She knew she would do it somehow, though, the same way she did everything she had to do. It was just another example of the Blakemores' overbearing attitude that Garrett would just step in and take over. And at the same time, it was the sweetest, most touching thing anyone had ever done for her, and she was desperately afraid she was going to burst into grateful tears.

"You must have something else to do today," she said, sounding wobbly despite her best intentions.

He shook his head, then bent to place the roller on the edge of the paint tray before crossing the room to her. "If I go back to Austin, I'll probably just go into the office," he said. "That's what I usually do on weekends. And the truth is, I don't need to. So I might as well stay here. I think I'd enjoy this more."

There was a sense of surprise in his voice at his own words. Lanie's heart quickened at the note of self-discovery, and she worked to block it out. She didn't dare let herself be drawn to him, to his sensitivity and kindness. There was too much at stake.

"I'm sure you could find some better way to amuse yourself than painting a room in my house," she said quickly.

"Do you argue with everyone who tries to help you, or just me?" he asked.

"Just you," she confessed.

He laughed. "I was afraid of that."

"Why are you doing this?" she couldn't help asking, and she found herself holding her breath while she waited for his answer.

He stared at her for a long, quiet moment. "Because you're family, if nothing else, Lanie. And because I want to."

If nothing else?

His words spun around in her head. What in the world did that mean?

"All right," she said, eager suddenly to just end the conversation. He was confusing her, and she didn't want to be confused. She wanted to think straight, and that meant not staying in the same room with Garrett. "I'd better take Dalton out of here, though. He shouldn't be around the paint fumes.'' She hesitated. ''I, uh, I'll bring you a glass of lemonade.''

Garrett watched Lanie run away before he set back to work. He had no doubt that was what she was doing. Running. From him. Because she was as finished with him as he was with her—which was not at all.

He didn't understand her, or the way she made him feel, he only knew he couldn't stay away. He'd gone halfway around the globe and hadn't gotten her out of his mind. He'd been drawn back to her as if pulled by an invisible string. There was still the question of Ben's baby, but there was more now, too. Much more.

It'd been a shock, his first look at her. At least when she was pregnant, it had been easier for him to remember that the erotic thoughts she'd incited even then were inappropriate.

There was nothing so clear to flash that warning at him anymore.

She was more beautiful than ever. Slender now with gentle curves, wearing impossibly short shorts and a cropped yellow T-shirt, she'd taken his breath away. She didn't look anything like a mom. She looked too young to be a mother, for one thing. Younger than her twenty-five years. But when he looked into her eyes, he saw pain and pride and a mature emotion that made him want to run for the hills and fold her into his arms, all at the same time.

It was a more-subtle sort of warning, and one he

couldn't heed—because he couldn't get her out of his mind. He had to face down the mystery that was Lanie, for his own peace of mind. And for Walter's, too. His uncle was agitated, to say the least, about Lanie's continuing disregard for his demands.

Garrett worked for a good hour on the room, and finished the first wall. There hadn't been a sign of Lanie, or any sound from the baby, either.

Curious and a little concerned, he set the roller on the tray and went downstairs. He stopped short as he entered the parlor. Lanie sat, head lolled back to expose the soft line of her neck, in the rocking chair. Dalton slept in her arms. The bright morning had grown cloudy, and in the muted light Garrett watched the gentle rise and fall of her breathing.

He felt again the longing that had seized him when he'd first arrived, only more fiercely than before. God help him, he wanted her.

He wished he could feel a pure lust for her, but he didn't. It was complicated by an unsettling tenderness that bothered him even more than the lust.

Her lashes fluttered then, and she opened her eyes. He watched as she slowly focused on him, blinked.

"Oh, I was going to bring you lemonade," she said softly. "I'm sorry. I fell asleep."

"Don't apologize. I can get my own lemonade. I'm glad you're sleeping." He nodded at the baby. "Looks like you both need the rest. Don't get up," he told her when she looked as if she might.

"I feel bad with you up there working on my house," she said. "I could probably put Dalton back in his crib. He still has his days and nights mixed up to some extent, and he doesn't sleep too much at night."

"Which means you don't, either," Garrett said. "Please, sleep. Okay?"

She looked as if she was going to argue, and he was glad when she didn't. He didn't want to fight with Lanie anymore. *Make love, not war,* the old slogan popped uninvited into his mind. And of course, he couldn't get it out.

"Okay." Lanie looked grateful, and a little embarrassed and wary, too. "Thanks." She pressed the floor with her toes and started to rock again, snuggling the baby close in her arms.

Garrett went on to the kitchen, working hard to block the images of what it might be like if he were the one snuggling with Lanie, sleeping with Lanie, feeling that soft breathing against his chest, tangling his limbs with hers, and staying that way all night long.

He wasn't successful.

She made him lunch.

"Do you really work weekends all the time?" she asked him as she sliced tomatoes for sandwiches. Dalton gurgled from a baby swing in the corner.

She'd insisted he sit at the kitchen table and let

her wait on him—to make up for him insisting she sleep all morning with Dalton while he painted.

"Don't you have any hobbies?" she persisted.

Garrett contemplated his personal life, away from work. It was basically nonexistent, and that hadn't bothered him before. He recalled how strange he'd felt earlier when he'd admitted to Lanie that he didn't really need to work on the weekends. Whether he needed to work on the weekends or not had never been the point before. Going to the office on Saturday was just part of his routine. He'd picked up the habit from Walter. It was simply a good work ethic.

But he knew he could cut back, if he wanted to. If he had a reason to.

"What do you usually do on the weekends?" he countered, turning the question around on her.

"With a bed-and-breakfast, weekends are when I get most of my business," she pointed out. "But I'm often free during the week, which can be nice. I volunteer at the elementary school—I help run the reading program. I'm on the visitors' committee with the chamber of commerce, too, and I work on the various festivals and events in town. I used to teach swimming lessons at the city pool every summer, but I'm going to have to skip that this year. I'm not getting near a bathing suit anytime soon."

The image of Lanie in a bikini sprang unbidden into Garrett's mind. He was instantly hot and uncomfortable, despite the pleasant temperature inside the house.

"I didn't realize you were so involved in the community," he said firmly, working to focus on something that wouldn't fuel his desire.

Lanie shrugged, continued building their sandwiches. "I haven't been very involved lately," she said. "But things will get back to normal, after Dalton gets a little older, settles into a schedule. I like working in the community. Deer Creek has given a lot to me, and I want to give back. I didn't have many relatives as a kid, and growing up in Deer Creek was like growing up in one big family. Everyone watches out for each other here."

Garrett wondered what it would be like to feel that sort of bond with a place. It was impossible for him to imagine. He'd lived in Austin most of his life and had never felt it. And he hadn't realized he was missing anything—until now.

Lanie set a plate in front of him, piled with two sandwiches and a mound of potato chips. She sat down across from him.

"Where's the furniture for the room?" he asked after a few minutes.

"It's in the garage," she explained. "There are some pretty heavy pieces, but Patty's husband, Trent, offered to carry it up. It'll take more than him, but I can round up a friend."

"I'm more than halfway done painting. If you can have him come over this evening before I leave, I can help him carry it up."

He wanted to be the *friend* she turned to when

she needed help. Maybe if he focused on being her friend, he'd get over his other feelings.

"Thank you." She finished her sandwich and made the call from a cordless phone she brought into the kitchen. "Trent and Patty will be over later," she told him when she hung up.

Garrett set his plate in the sink. "Great."

She stood there, her fingers jammed into the little front pockets of her shorts, staring at him. "I— you're being awfully nice," she said.

"Wasn't I nice before?"

She lifted a brow, didn't answer.

"That was my evil twin. I'm the good twin."

She didn't even crack a smile.

"Look I'm just waiting for the other shoe to drop, that's all," she said. The steady hum of the battery-powered baby swing was the only sound for a seemingly timeless beat. "I've been getting letters from your uncle's attorney—"

"Letters you've ignored. I know all about that." Garrett sobered. "But that's not why I'm here."

"Then why? Why are you here? You didn't come to paint my room and move my furniture."

"I came to see Dalton," he said, moving cautiously through an explanation that was only part of the truth. "I've been thinking about him."

"Thinking about him?"

"I'd like to see him, every once in a while." He realized, over the past few weeks, that whether he could or should walk away from Lanie and the feelings she inspired, there was something he *couldn't* walk away from.

"You're asking for some kind of visitation?" she asked dubiously.

"Nothing formal," he said. "I'd just like to see him. If this is Ben's baby—"

He hesitated, seeing her flinch at his use of the word *if* and feeling crazily guilty. He forced himself to go on, to disregard her hurt.

"If this is Ben's baby, then I have an obligation to Ben to do something to fill the role he's left vacant."

"I have friends, lots of friends," Lanie said hurriedly. "You don't have to worry that Dalton will lack for male role models."

"That doesn't change the fact that I have an obligation to Ben."

He walked closer to her. She shifted backward, and he followed her. She bumped up against the kitchen counter and stopped, her gaze flashing nervously to his.

Stepping toward her again, he deliberately invaded her comfort zone. Was she nervous because he was discussing visitation with Dalton, or because of his physical proximity to her at this moment?

"So if Dalton is Ben's child," he pressed, "then it would follow that I have an obligation to Dalton, too, don't you think?"

"I—I guess."

Her voice came out wispy. She was flushed, and

he could see a pulse beating frantically at the base of her throat.

"Good," he said slowly, watching the quick dart of her tongue as she wet her lips. "So it's settled."

Then he turned and strode out of the room before he settled the other thing—whether or not she wanted to kiss him as much as he wanted to kiss her.

Chapter Nine

The old door on Lanie's detached garage screeched in protest as Garrett pushed it up. Lanie flicked on the interior light. The musty closed-in air met the damp dusk. Rumbles from the thick, dark cloud-bank overhead reminded everyone that time was of the essence. The air was heavy with the scent of rain.

"We'd better get after this—it's fixing to pour," Trent Spencer, Patty's husband, said.

"Just point out which boxes and which pieces of furniture you want, and we'll take it from there," Garrett said to Lanie.

She steadied her gaze on him. "The more of us working, the better, I don't want things getting wet. I told you before, I'm perfectly fine. There's no reason for me not to help carry stuff in."

She breezed past him and picked up a box. The three of them made several trips back and forth, while Patty took care of Dalton inside. Patty had tried to get Lanie to switch with her—Lanie stay inside and watch Dalton while Patty did the work—but Lanie had been determined not to sit idly by and let her friends put in all the effort.

And she was equally determined not to let Garrett dictate her activity. She hadn't felt as if she'd had a real choice when he'd declared his intention to fill a role in Dalton's life. But she did have a choice in how much of a role Garrett played in *her* life. He had no business telling her what to do.

And she had no business fantasizing about kissing him, she reminded herself. She'd almost melted in the kitchen earlier, under his close regard.

She still felt shivery when she thought about it. And she kept thinking about it, even though she tried very hard not to.

After they'd carried in all the boxes, they came to the heavy antique furniture. Garrett put his hand on her arm. ''I don't care what you say, it's only been four weeks since you had a baby. You're going to carry this furniture over my dead body.''

Just his brief touch was enough to make her start melting again.

She countered the reaction with deliberate flippancy. ''Hmm. Now you're tempting me.''

Garrett watched her with such intensity that her words evolved to a meaning she hadn't intended, and she could hardly breathe for a few seconds.

Then he spoke, breaking the spell. "Do you think you could just let me do you one favor without having to fight for it?"

She swallowed, focused. She knew he was right about her carrying the furniture, but she wasn't going to give him the satisfaction of saying so.

"Okay, fine," she said instead. "You can do me this favor. But next time, we fight." She couldn't help enjoying the surprised swirl of light she glimpsed in his eyes just before she spun around on her heel and marched back to the house.

Her heart drummed wildly. She felt breathless. What was she doing? She'd come dangerously close to *flirting* with Garrett, for heaven's sake. Flirting! She shouldn't be doing that—only, right then, she was having a hard time remembering exactly why. She felt such a rush of heat and desire, it clouded her mind.

Patty was waiting for her in the kitchen, pacing and patting a fussy Dalton.

"Oh, thank goodness," Patty said. "This baby wants his mommy." She handed him over. He quieted right away once in Lanie's arms.

Lanie patted his back and murmured softly in Dalton's ear. She went to the kitchen window and looked outside toward the garage where Trent and Garrett worked. She watched Garrett heft a headboard into his arms. His strong muscles drew her eyes.

She almost jumped out of her skin when Patty suddenly spoke.

"So tell me about Garrett."

Lanie looked at her friend blankly. "He's Ben's cousin."

"I know *that*. And I know all about how he came here demanding tests and ended up taking you to the hospital. But you made him sound like a jerk. Are you sure this is the same guy?"

"He is being kind of…nice, isn't he?" What was she saying? She shook herself. "I think it's because he wants visitation with Dalton. He thinks he has an obligation to Ben to—I don't know. Play some sort of fatherly role in Dalton's life."

"Oh, really?" Patty lifted her brow. "Well, that's awfully commendable."

Lanie could see Patty's opinion of Garrett was moving up several notches.

Garrett arrived at the back door. Lanie held the door open, then followed upstairs to direct placement of the furniture he and Trent carried up over the next several trips between the garage and the house. Patty joined in to help the men, and the room filled quickly. Lanie found herself bumping into Garrett more than once in the jam of unpacked boxes and furniture. The electric current of the contact took her breath away and spurred powerful images that she would have been better off without.

She ordered pizza, and the delivery arrived as the men brought in the last load. It started raining at the same time. Dalton was hungry, and crying up a storm of his own by then, so she went upstairs to nurse him.

When she came back down, having left Dalton tucked in his crib, she found everyone in the back den, an area she kept private from bed-and-breakfast guests. It was comfortable and messy, full of worn furniture and shelves stacked with old magazines and books. Photos filled the walls. She hadn't changed it since her grandmother's death, and it was so cozy, she doubted she ever would. The TV was back here, and she could see that was what had drawn everyone. A baseball game filled the small screen. Pizza boxes lay open on the coffee table along with glasses and a pitcher of iced lemonade. Outside, rain pounded down in the pitch dark.

She stood in the doorway for a minute, soaking in the easy atmosphere in the room, and how Garrett fit in with her friends. She'd seen the way he and Trent had been joking around while they'd hauled in her things. Now Garrett was arguing amiably with Patty over one of the ballplayer's merits.

Lanie moved into the room. "Hey, what's the score?"

She'd brought the baby monitor down so she could hear if Dalton woke. Setting it on the coffee table, she slipped to a cross-legged position on the floor. She poured herself a glass of lemonade, then reached for a warm, gooey slice of pizza.

Garrett looked at her, and their eyes locked. Her tummy did a little flip. He gave her the score, in his deep, even voice. But he wasn't thinking about baseball when he looked at her, she was sure of it.

She'd started something out there when she'd half-way flirted with him—and he hadn't forgotten it.

How could she have been so reckless?

Because she wanted him, the answer came, and it frightened her more than a little. Was it just a physical thing, an awakening of her womanly center after her body had been pregnant and lumbering for all those months? If so, why couldn't she find someone more suitable?

"We should get going," Patty said abruptly. "It's really coming down out there, and I just remembered I opened our bedroom window this morning when it was so nice, and I never went back to shut it. I bet there's water all over the rug."

She stood, and Trent followed her lead.

"Oh no." Lanie felt the urge to throw her arms around Patty and Trent's knees like a three-year-old and beg them to stay.

She didn't want to be alone with Garrett. She was afraid her control was starting to slip.

"Don't get up," Patty admonished her when she started to rise. "We know our way out."

She and Trent said their goodbyes to Garrett, and a minute later Lanie heard the front door close.

"I like your friends," Garrett commented.

Lanie swallowed a bite of pizza. "Thanks. They're great."

She pretended to pay attention to the game for a few minutes while she consumed another slice of pizza and downed half her glass of lemonade. The storm picked up, and she could hear the wind howling down the chimney in the parlor. Thunder rattled the windows. Lightning flashed across the sky.

"I hope Patty and Trent are home by now." Lanie looked at Garrett, and it suddenly occurred to her that he was going to be driving home soon, too. And he had a lot farther to go than Patty and Trent. As much as she needed him to leave, the thought of him on a dark highway in this downpour disturbed her.

"Maybe you should stay until this lets up," she said, and then there was a pop and the electricity went off. The TV screen receded to a tiny dot of light then disappeared completely.

"So much for the game," Garrett said lightly.

"I think I've got some candles and matches in the kitchen." She got up and started moving blindly through the familiar layout of the house.

Somebody had left one of the kitchen chairs pulled out, and Lanie learned about it the hard way when she nearly half fell over it. "Ouch!"

"Lanie?" Garrett called from the other room.

"I'm okay," she called back.

She made her way by touch to the top drawer by the refrigerator and located the necessary items. The scratch of the match was barely audible over successive booms of thunder.

Candleholder in hand, she turned and had a head-on collision with Garrett. She gasped and jumped back from the accidental contact.

"I didn't mean to startle you," he said. "I just came to make sure you were all right."

The candle spread a surreal haze of golden light over the room, softening Garrett's hard features. Softening more than that, too—she felt weak with a heat that came out of nowhere.

"I'm okay, I told you. I just stumbled over one of the kitchen chairs."

"Are you sure you're not hurt?" he asked. "You're trembling."

She looked down at her hands. She *was* trembling. The candle shook visibly.

"I'm not hurt," she said.

"Are you nervous?" His voice sounded husky and strange to her ears. Different.

Was his heart beating as fast as hers?

"Storms make me nervous," she said.

"Really?" He moved incrementally nearer. "It's the storm, not me?"

His eyes roamed her face. Her heart palpitated irregularly in response.

For a wild instant she wondered if he was going to kiss her. Her traitorous heart sang and danced at the thought. She wanted him to kiss her.

She wanted—needed—to touch him, taste him. It was a lilting, heady, mind-blowing need.

"I should check on Dalton," she said breathlessly, skirting around him. "I'm afraid the storm will have woken him." She needed to bring down the crackling heat between them, and she hoped desperately that the baby was awake to do the job.

Garrett sat down at the kitchen table. "Wasn't that a baby monitor you brought down with you?"

"Oh." So much for that escape plan. "Good point."

She went to the den to fetch it.

"He's not making a peep, if you can believe that," she reported as she arrived back in the kitchen with the monitor in one hand, the candle in the other. "If I so much as breathe sometimes, I wake him up. But he sleeps through all this." She sat across the table from Garrett, placing the candle and monitor between them. "I can get the radio if you want to listen to the game, keep up with the score. I haven't used it on battery power since last summer, but the batteries should still be good."

She was babbling and she knew it, but the combination of candlelight and Garrett was really a little too much. Spring storms usually passed quickly, and she could only hope this one would run true to form.

"Do you want to keep up with the game?" he asked.

"Uh, well, no. Actually I don't like listening to sports that much," she admitted.

"What do you like?"

She liked the way his mouth curved in that sexy, sardonic way when he spoke. She liked the way he leaned forward, resting his elbows on the table, watching her as if she were the most fascinating person in the world.

"Gardening and baking," she said slowly, working to jerk herself out of the hypnotic power of his nearness. "Soap operas and country music. Am I boring you yet?"

Maybe she could convince him that she was the dullest creature on Earth, and then he would stop looking at her in that way that made her feel boneless.

"No." Garrett didn't find anything about Lanie boring. He could see the tiredness in her eyes. Her hair looked messy, and her makeup was nonexistent. But she was beautiful. She was natural and real, and he'd never been so attracted to a woman in his life. The innocent way she'd teased him earlier had driven him crazy. "I think you're very interesting."

"You do spend too much time at the office, don't you?" she joked.

She changed the subject then, and started talking about the weather. She told him about a storm the year before that had knocked down her favorite pecan tree in the backyard. There was a thread of nervousness in her voice that made him think she wasn't comfortable sitting in the candlelight with a man.

It was more of that elusive innocence he sensed in her—elusive because it wasn't based on anything factual, just on feeling.

When she paused, he asked her bluntly, "Are you seeing anyone?"

She looked confused at the subject switch. "Seeing anyone?"

"Dating anyone?"

"Oh, sure." Her gaze was wary. "You've seen

the men lining up at the door, right? Babies are such a turn-on." She shrugged. "I'm not looking for a relationship, anyway. Dalton is the number-one man in my life now. His needs come first. I have to be very careful about bringing someone into our lives."

"Careful?"

"I would never want to be with someone who couldn't care for Dalton as his own," she said plainly. "That's more important than anything else. I want Dalton to feel loved, always."

"What about you?" he couldn't resist asking, tantalized by the ever-present curiosity he felt about her. "Is that what you want?"

She tilted her head. "Isn't that what everyone wants, to be loved?"

He stared at her. For a full minute there was nothing but the sounds of rain lashing down outside and the sudden heavy beating of his heart.

"It's a pretty intangible emotion, don't you think?" he asked finally. "It's fine for stories and songs, but it's not reality."

"I don't agree," she argued. "Love *is* tangible. It's support and faith, comfort and encouragement. It's the small acts that make up everyday life. It's very real. Haven't you ever been in love?"

"I've been married."

"That's not necessarily the same thing."

"That, I can agree with," he said dryly.

"Was your marriage that bad?"

He didn't mince words. "I came home early one day and found her in bed with somebody else."

Compassion filled her sweet blue eyes. "That's terrible."

"That's life," he countered. Her sympathy made him uncomfortable. "Love, trust—that's the stuff of fairy tales." He sounded cynical even to himself. "It ends badly more than half the time. Don't you watch the news?"

Thunder rumbled, this time from farther away. He realized the rain was slackening, and he was sorry, because he would have no more excuse to stay. He didn't want to leave. But he had to, before he did something stupid. Like start believing in fairy tales.

The electricity snapped back on. The refrigerator hummed to life, and sound and light from the den spilled into the kitchen.

"The electricity's back on," Lanie said, completely unnecessarily. She felt inexplicably depressed. "The storm's letting up," she added.

Garrett was silent for a moment. "I should go," he said. "I'm sure you want to get some sleep before the baby wakes."

She rose, leaving the candle on the table. "Thanks for all your help today," she said stiffly. She led the way to the front door, letting the faint glow from the den illuminate their path.

She stopped at the door and turned, stared at him in the shadows.

He was right behind her.

"Drive carefully," she said.

He didn't move for long seconds. His dark eyes searched hers. Then he touched her face, drew the back of his knuckles along her cheekbone, and brushed her lips with his thumb. The contact was firm but gentle, and it sent a flood of erotic messages through her treacherously responsive body.

"Maybe I'm the one who's wrong," he said softly, sliding his hand to her neck, into her hair. Tingles of sensual anticipation lit up her nerve ends. "Maybe I'm just jaded. You deserve your fairy tales."

She stared at him. His mouth came closer, and her insides started liquifying at an alarming rate. "Love isn't a fairy tale," she whispered, desperate for a foothold in sanity. He moved an increment nearer. It wasn't fair that she wanted him this much, that he could make her feel this way. Where was the justice in the world?

"You make me want to believe that," he said. "You make me want—" And then he didn't finish because he was kissing her.

Chapter Ten

She tasted like lemonade and hope. Soft and warm, she fit perfectly in his arms. Garrett felt Lanie's hesitation, then her surrender—and it intoxicated him, dissolving him into fiery heat and need that made no excuses, asked for no explanations. She relaxed against him, her arms slipping around his neck. She met the teasing, demanding exploration of his tongue as he immediately deepened the kiss.

Desire streaked through his body, stronger and more powerful than he'd ever known. The tiniest thread of control held him back from scooping her into his arms and carrying her upstairs to any one of the big, soft beds he knew were up there.

He felt like the young man he'd once been, full of optimism and a belief that anything was possible. His mouth wandered from the sweetness of her lips to the silky line of her jaw, to her neck. With his tongue, he drew a line up to her ear and elicited a low moan from her throat that drove him wild. He groaned in response, buried his fingers in her hair, holding her even closer.

He wanted more, much more. And if he wasn't mistaken, so did she. He wanted to bury himself in the reckless physical need he felt for her—bury himself so deep, the emotional need he was fast developing for her would be engulfed.

"Lanie," he whispered raspily against her ear. "I can't believe how much I want you."

Lanie drew back and stared at Garrett. Her breaths came in quick little gasps. Electric desire was buzzing to every nerve end of her body. He felt so good, so right, and his words were like magic.

He wanted her.

She wanted him, too—so much that she couldn't even think. And that scared her.

"Lanie, I—"

"No. Stop." She wrenched out of his arms and stood cold and shuddering before him.

"What is it? What's wrong?"

Everything, she wanted to shout.

"We shouldn't be doing this."

"Why not? You told me you aren't seeing anyone. We're two unattached adults—"

"That doesn't make it right. Do you go around kissing every unattached adult you come across?" She tried to make her words sound light, but her lips felt swollen and she ached to be back in his arms.

Garrett stared at her. "No, of course I don't go around kissing every unattached adult I come across." His mouth quirked. "Only the women."

She crossed her arms tightly, protectively. "Okay, laugh all you want."

He grew serious immediately. "I'm not laughing at *you*." He touched her chin, gently forcing her gaze to lock with his. "I'm sorry, Lanie. I was sure you wanted that kiss as much as I did. I would never have done it otherwise."

She shivered beneath his scrutiny, his touch. How could she deny it? Her response to him had been easily evident.

"I thought you were here to see Dalton," she said weakly, struggling to find something coherent to say as she backed away from his touch. "I just don't think it would be a good idea if we—"

She broke off, still struggling. "We've both had difficult experiences in the past," she went on. "Probably neither one of us is ready for a relationship right now." She was afraid Garrett would never be ready for a relationship. And she wasn't ready for heartbreak. "I don't think it would be a good idea for us to get involved…physically. This situation is complicated enough, don't you think?"

He was silent for a long moment, then he nodded. "You're right. We shouldn't get involved. Dalton comes first." He took a deep breath, studied her.

"I apologize for kissing you. It was a presumptuous and irresponsible thing to do."

He sounded very formal suddenly, his eyes had gone cold, shuttered, desolate. She wanted to cry for no sensible reason.

"It's okay," she whispered. "It was—"

Nothing. She'd been going to say his kiss was nothing. But she couldn't get the word out.

"About Dalton," he said stiffly. "He's only a baby now, but I want him to know who I am, be familiar with me. I want to see him on a regular basis."

Lanie nodded. Her throat felt too full to try to speak.

"I'd like to come back next Saturday afternoon, if that's okay. The weather's been nice. I'm not sure what you do with babies, but I noticed a park a couple blocks from here. Maybe I could take him for a walk. Does he have a stroller?"

"Yes. That would be fine."

He watched her. "I don't think I'm ready to be alone with him yet. I'm not used to being around babies. If you could come with us, it would make me feel a lot better. I'll stop by the deli and pick up a picnic basket, if that sounds all right."

He let his words hang there.

"Oh." Comprehension dawned. "All right." But it wasn't all right. How was she going to spend time with Garrett when she was crazy with desire for him? She needed to get away from Garrett, far away.

But at the same time, she knew that this was what she'd wanted when she'd initially contacted Walter. She'd wanted a relationship for Dalton with his father's family. The important thing for herself to remember was to not inject too much meaning into Garrett's interest. It didn't mean he trusted her, that he absolutely believed Dalton was Ben's baby. It just meant he wanted to spend time with Dalton, that was all.

She knew the issue of the testing was still out there, waiting. And for all she knew, Garrett's interest in spending time with Dalton was but a ruse to pressure her into the testing—and then pressure her into who knew what afterward. She could be giving Walter—through Garrett—a dangerous foothold in Dalton's life. She was afraid, but what choice did she have? She would just take things one step at a time, make careful decisions and see what happened. It was all she could do.

If only she could be certain that Walter wouldn't make undue demands on her, on Dalton, she would have gone ahead and gotten the testing over with by now—just to eliminate the irritation of Walter's demands. But while the initial shock and offense of the request had worn off, her wariness had not. She felt vulnerable, one woman against a powerful man like Walter Blakemore with all his money and his legion of attorneys. It was important to establish that *she* was going to be in charge of Dalton, not Walter.

She watched Garrett drive away, her fingers

pressed to her still-trembling lips. She was doing the right thing. The right thing for Dalton, taking one tiny, careful step toward a relationship with his father's family.

And if it took every ounce of strength inside her spirit, she was going to make sure it didn't turn out to be the wrong thing for *her*.

He called midweek.

"Dalton has his first cold," she told him. "I took him to church on Sunday, and everyone wanted to coo over him. Now he's sniffling and feverish." She rushed on with the rest of it, her speech well rehearsed. "He'll probably be better by the weekend, but I don't think I'd feel right about taking him out again—even just to the park."

She refused to think about the fact that she was just scared because she wanted Garrett so much, and that she was making too much of Dalton's cold—latching on to it like a lifeboat.

Wasn't it a mother's prerogative to fuss over her baby's first illness, no matter how minor?

Delaying seeing Garrett again only delayed the inevitable. But she was delaying, anyway.

"Is he all right?" he asked, concern infused in his voice. "Have you taken him to the doctor?"

"I called his pediatrician. I don't need to take him in unless his fever goes up. It's just one of those things—it'll take a few days to run its course and then he'll be fine. Don't worry."

He asked a few more questions, then he hung up

without making alternative plans. She wondered if he was losing interest already. How serious was his commitment to Dalton? Garrett was a busy man.

It was for the best, she told herself. So why was she so disappointed?

Garrett put down the phone, stared out the wide windows of his Austin office. The Blakemore Corporation was located in a prestigious downtown business district. He enjoyed the view and the energy of the city around him. He enjoyed his work, too. The aggressive business of acquisitions and mergers had fueled him for so long he couldn't remember when it hadn't.

It was his whole life. The challenge kindled his blood.

Lanie's beautiful face hovered in his mind. Was that what drove his hunger for her? Challenge? The need to possess what was not yet in his grasp?

Or was it…something else? Could he be falling in love with her?

How could he fall in love when he didn't believe in it? Much less with a woman he wasn't even sure he could trust?

He was supposed to be focusing on Dalton. He'd almost lost control when he'd kissed Lanie, and that would have been a mistake.

Since he'd turned over the issue of Dalton's testing to Walter's attorney, he'd tried to shove it from his mind. But he couldn't help wondering…

Was he setting himself up to be made a fool of…yet again? Lanie tempted him, lured him.

When he was with her, there was something alive in him that hadn't been alive in a long time. It was something he barely recognized, something that had been walled over one brick at a time since he was nine years old and had learned that his parents were dead.

The wall had become complete the day he'd walked in and found Vanessa in another man's arms. Now there was a breach in that wall, a brick pulled loose.

And through that crevice he felt his heart. It was alive and beating despite all his neglect, and it was telling him something.

Did he dare listen?

Saturday evening, Lanie slipped Dalton gently into his crib and stared down at his tiny sleeping form. He was such a miracle. She smiled in spite of the doldrums she'd been wallowing in for days.

Garrett hadn't called back, hadn't suggested another visitation with Dalton. It was for the best, she repeated her now-familiar mantra.

She walked back downstairs. Late-afternoon golden light striped the house. With the baby asleep, it was the perfect time for her to do something useful, like organize her books. Or her kitchen drawers. Anything to take her mind off what she *might* have been doing this evening—spending time with Garrett.

It was time for her to forget about Garrett Blakemore for good.

A knock brought her around. She went to the front door.

"Hello," Garrett said with a big, sexy smile, his dark eyes gleaming. He held a large picnic hamper in one arm and a teddy bear in the other. He wore jeans and a spiffy Western-style shirt that was, of course, perfectly ironed.

She took it all in, her mind spinning. Her own attire registered with a jolt. She was wearing a hip-length ivory nightie under an equally brief matching robe, with fluffy slippers on her feet and her hair scraped back into a French braid.

She stood there, looking at him blankly, a slow wave of embarrassment warming her face. Trying not to be too obvious about it, she felt for the sash and tied the robe together.

"How's Dalton?" Garrett asked, displaying no evidence in his tone that he noticed her apparel, but a certain hot, hungry light in his eyes as he looked at her added to her discomfort.

She worked to act completely natural. "He's still sniffly, but his fever is down."

"Good." He smiled again. "I'm glad to hear that," he added.

"He's sleeping right now."

"Can I come in?" he asked.

"Okay." She moved aside to let him enter.

He handed her the bear. "This is for Dalton."

She accepted the gift. "Thank you." She remembered how she'd cried over a cookie commercial when she was five months pregnant. She felt the same way right now, about Garrett and his teddy bear. He hadn't forgotten about Dalton, hadn't lost interest.

"What are you doing here?" she asked him finally, struggling not to get any more sappy and silly than she already was. She was, she decided, definitely experiencing postpartum hormones.

"We had plans for a picnic," he pointed out. His gaze raked her. She could see an amused, intrigued flash in his dark eyes when they returned to lock on hers. "Did you forget?"

"No, I thought—" She broke off, wrapping her arms tight around herself. "I thought it was off."

"I knew you didn't want to take him out to the park today," he said, "but I was hoping we could have our picnic here. If that's okay."

It wasn't okay. It wasn't okay at all—because every time she looked at him, all she could think about was how it had felt to kiss him. But she couldn't explain that, so she had to say, "Of course," and start praying for selective amnesia.

Chapter Eleven

Lanie smoothed her hands down the sides of her shrimp-colored blouse, tucking the soft material into the waistband of white shorts. She scrutinized herself in the full-length antique mirror in her bedroom. Outside, Garrett was setting up the picnic he'd brought, while she'd gone upstairs to get dressed. She'd taken down her hair, combed it out into thick waves that whispered over her bare shoulders.

She turned to the side, ran her hand over her tummy with a critical eye. Her stomach would never be as flat as it had been before she'd carried Dalton. But she'd lost much of the baby weight, thanks to breast-feeding. Dalton was a big eater. What weight she hadn't lost added the fullness of curves where there hadn't been any before—her hips, her tummy, her breasts.

She had a woman's body now, not a girl's anymore. But she felt like a girl tonight, at least inside. A girl not more than sixteen. Her pulse raced, and flutters filled her stomach. Her cheeks flushed, her eyes glowed.

She felt shy and uncertain, full of anticipation.

It was Garrett. She was grateful for the attention he was giving Dalton, she told herself. But she knew that didn't completely explain her feelings.

Which meant she had a problem. A big problem.

Dalton was still sleeping soundly when she checked on him. She brought the baby monitor downstairs and picked up the portable radio on her way through the house. She found Garrett in the yard, spreading out a quilt she'd given him for that purpose. He'd chosen a flat spot beneath a tree. The sky was dusky, and the half-moon was already visible above them. The evening air was warm, but when he straightened and looked at her, with the branches of the tree casting shadows over his hard-planed features, she shivered.

"Hi." She let go of the screen door, then walked across the deck and onto the grass. "Dalton's still asleep. Hopefully, he'll be up soon."

"Great." He smiled at her.

She spoke again, nervous. "I brought the radio." She was afraid of being alone with Garrett and thought the boom box could fill any silences. She switched it on. It was on her usual country-western station. A fast-paced song poured out. She was grateful for the noise.

"Are you hungry?" Garrett asked.

"Yes, thanks." She sat, tucking her legs beneath her, and Garrett knelt to begin unloading the basket. It was filled with sandwiches, cold salads and soft drinks. He'd already brought out ice-filled glasses, plates and silverware from the kitchen. "I'm always starving lately," she said. "Because of the baby."

She was feeling light-headed, though she knew that wasn't because she was hungry. Her control was draining away. She needed to get it back, quickly.

Just as he handed her a plate, a wail came from the baby monitor. Lanie could have collapsed with relief. This whole setup was way too romantic.

"I'd better go get him." She started to get up, but Garrett wouldn't have it.

"Let me. If you don't mind?"

"Okay." She watched him as he strode back to the house, admiring his trim, muscular body, the calm authority with which he carried himself. A rush of physical attraction swept over her.

She took a gulp of her cold drink and thought about what a good thing it was that it wasn't alcoholic. As if she weren't intoxicated enough already, just looking at Garrett. But she had no business responding to him this way. Garrett's relationship was with Dalton, not with her.

A few minutes later, Garrett rejoined her, Dalton carefully balanced in the crook of his arm. The baby's face was starting to fill out, his cheeks plumping with health, his little eyes shining. His dark hair stood straight up from his head in fuzzy abandon. She'd dressed him in a one-piece snapped cotton outfit decorated with colorful dinosaurs. Settled in Garrett's arms, he cooed and blew bubbles and looked surprisingly content.

"Want me to take him?" she offered as Garrett reached her.

"He doesn't seem hungry, does he?" Garrett asked. "Is it all right if I keep the little guy for a while, until he needs you?"

"Oh. Okay."

She watched as Garrett sat down across from her, nimbly sliding Dalton up onto his shoulder, holding the baby with one strong hand while he picked up his drink with the other and took a sip.

She took a bite of her food. It was delicious, but she realized for once she wasn't hungry, even though she'd been telling Garrett the truth about her big appetite. But right now she was nervous and excited, and it was hard to concentrate on food.

"You looked so afraid of holding him the day he was born," she commented. "Now you look like a natural." The tender ease with which Garrett held her son made her eyes sting. It was sad, really sad, she thought suddenly, that Garrett seemed to have given up on love. He had the makings of a wonderful father.

It occurred to her that at this rate, it wouldn't be long before he was comfortable taking Dalton out for visits without her accompaniment. The thought depressed her.

"I wouldn't say I'm a natural, but I'm a fast learner," he said. He took a bite of his own food, juggling the baby to maneuver around him. After swallowing, he added, "This baby stuff is no big deal, right, slugger?"

He sent Lanie a warm, teasing grin.

"Oh, sure, you're not here at 2:00 a.m.," Lanie returned, trying to sound careless.

The offhand comment backfired when she saw the spark of heat flare in his eyes. No, he wasn't here at 2:00 a.m., but he wouldn't mind it and neither would she. She figured she'd taken a turn down a conversational road they didn't need to follow.

She tried to think of another topic, but then Dalton started to fuss a little, and she watched as Garrett put down his sandwich and with one strong hand supporting the baby's head, jiggled him very lightly. Dalton smiled, quieted, then in another second, spewed spit-up all over Garrett's front.

Lanie gasped. "Oh, no."

"Is something wrong with him?" Garrett asked, his face a mask of shock. He held the baby out in front of him, gaping down at his sodden lap.

"I'm so sorry!" Lanie leaned over, scooped up Dalton. "I'm sorry," she repeated. "Don't worry, there's nothing wrong with him. He does this all the time. It's just, you know, a baby thing."

"No, I didn't know."

He stood, unbuttoning and then stripping off his soaked shirt. Lanie scrambled up, Dalton still in her arms.

"I'll find you some clothes to wear," she offered. "I can go ahead and wash your shirt while you're here. And your pants."

"Uh, yeah, I'd appreciate that," he said dryly.

Lanie felt a gurgle in her throat, then she was laughing, she couldn't help it. And he was laughing, too, thank goodness.

"I'm sorry," she said, gasping out the words as she tried to get hold of herself, biting down on her lip to keep from laughing again.

Her gaze fell to Garrett's bare chest then, and a spear of desire settled within her. A slight scattering of dark fuzz covered his developed muscles. She looked up, found him watching her.

"We'd better get Dalton changed, and get those clothes in the wash," she said quickly. "Come on." She headed inside, glad to have something concrete with which to occupy herself. "I'm just really, really sorry this happened."

Garrett stopped her, reaching around to grip her arm. "Stop apologizing," he said firmly. "It's okay. Like you said, it's a baby thing. I don't mind."

"You don't mind baby spit-up? Even I mind baby spit-up and he's my—"

Garrett silenced her by touching his fingers softly to her mouth. The gesture was impossibly natural, as if they'd known each other for years. It was dreamy, intimate.

The moment grew even more dreamy when he leaned in, closer, his thumb rubbing down along her jaw, and she thought he was going to kiss her again, and then Dalton squawked, cocooned as he was between them. Garrett dropped his hand, stepped back.

Lanie felt like she was going to die, she was so disappointed. It took her a couple of dizzy seconds to remember what she was supposed to be doing. Laundry. She was going to find some clothes for Garrett and wash his soiled things.

"Okay, wait here while I get some fresh clothes," she said and took off upstairs. She changed Dalton into a clean outfit in his room and brought down a T-shirt and pair of shorts for Garrett from one of the boxes of Ben's things.

Garrett changed quickly in the downstairs bathroom, then took Dalton outside while Lanie set the controls on the laundry machine.

When she came back out, she found Garrett dancing with Dalton beneath the tree. He whirled slowly to the music from the radio, the baby braced carefully against his chest. Dalton squealed, his big eyes bright and happy.

She stood just outside the back door, watching Garrett with her son. A blossom of emotion spread out from her heart, unfolding to every part of her body.

Instinctively, she didn't want to name the emotion. But not naming it didn't make it any less real. The knowledge brought with it a tremble of trepidation—and a thrill of elation at the same time.

What was she going to do? Every moment she

spent with Garrett was dangerous. She kept thinking about how he'd said she made him want to believe in fairy tales. Could she make him believe in love again?

She pressed her hand to her lips. It was a crazy thought. Insane. So why was it so hard to dismiss?

Garrett saw her then and he stopped, walked across to her with Dalton. The baby reached his arms up at her, and she took him. Her mind was still spinning with confusing feelings, and she needed something to focus on. Luckily, there was still dinner.

"Okay, I really am starving now," she announced, and settled down on the quilt again. They ate, listening to the radio and talking about casual things while Dalton gurgled from her lap.

Garrett asked her about the deck, and she told him how she'd had it built last year, though it was still incomplete. The lawn swept downward from the house, leaving a slight dropoff at the edge of the wooden structure. She kept hoping she'd have the funds to expand the deck, add a second tier with railings. She had a lot of plans.

She wondered where Garrett would fit into her plans, her future. Or if he would fit in at all.

Later she went inside to tuck Garrett's clothes into the dryer and to take a few minutes to feed the baby in private. When she came back out, Garrett was sitting on the love-seat-size glider on the deck. She joined him there, propping Dalton across her legs, and breathed in the fresh night.

"Dalton's going to be getting sleepy soon, I think," she said. "Do you want to rock him up-stairs in his room before you leave?"

"Thanks. Yes."

"Okay. Your things will be dry in a little while."

"This has been nice," he commented after a few minutes.

Garrett knew as he said it that he was making a vast understatement. He couldn't remember when he'd enjoyed an evening this much. With Lanie, he appreciated the simple things in life, like a baby's smile.

She made him feel alive. And the funny thing was, he hadn't even realized he was dead. Not until he'd set eyes on her. That was when it had started. Right then, the second she'd opened her door that first day.

"Baby spit-up and all?" Lanie probed, smiling her angel smile.

"Yep." He reached over and squeezed her hand briefly in his. She stared at him, her wide eyes suddenly serious and afraid. He let go of her hand, realizing instinctively that his touch was what caused her reaction. "It was just a touch, Lanie, that's all. No kissing, I know that. I remember the rules." He tried to make light of things between them. "Of course, if you change your mind and want to kiss, I'm always available," he said, and he was only half teasing.

"Stop it." She hit him in the arm, her words playful, though her eyes remained nervous. "I just want to be sure we remember what's important here. Dalton. This isn't about you and me."

He agreed with her intellectually, though he wondered if it was already too late. If it was already just as much about himself and Lanie as it was about Dalton.

"We have to learn to work together for Dalton's best interests," she remarked. She sounded very prim and purposeful. He noticed she wasn't looking him in the eye.

"What is it that scares you so much about kissing me?" he asked, determined to not be diverted.

She looked him in the eye then. "What?"

"What's wrong with kissing?" he probed. "It's a natural human instinct." And he was chock-full of natural human instinct.

"I don't know what you mean," she said, looking even more skittish than before.

"I mean kissing, like this." And before she could move, he dipped his head and placed his lips on hers, gently, and then drew back. "See? It's just a kiss. Nothing to be scared of." It struck him that they needed to get this attraction out in the open, stop hiding from it. He'd been hiding from so many feelings for so long. He didn't want to hide anymore. Lanie made him want to explore, to feel.

She was just staring at him, her eyes huge and dark in the falling night. He leaned in and captured her mouth again, devouring her this time, and she didn't resist. He wanted to drive out her hesitation, her fears—the way she drove out his—in an explosion of incendiary passion. The low, sexy sound she made, the capitulation to his sensual plunder, sent his head spinning. He knew what he needed—heart-stopping, mind-blowing, shockingly intense sex. And he needed it with Lanie.

Then she tore her mouth away. "No, stop," she breathed, and suddenly she was pushing at him with her hands against his chest.

"Why?" he demanded, his heart racing.

"Because I don't kiss men I'm not having a relationship with," she said, panic flaring in her eyes as she clutched at Dalton, pulling him out of her lap and up to her heaving breast. "And we've already established we're not having a relationship."

"Maybe it's time to reevaluate," he countered, working to steady his own raging pulse. "Look, I'm serious about getting to know Dalton, which means you and I are going to be spending some time together. It's silly for us to pretend we're not attracted to each other, don't you think? Can we just stop pretending? That's all I'm suggesting."

Lanie stared at Garrett, uncertain how to respond. She wanted to throw caution to the winds, but she was afraid.

"I'm not sure I understand what you're saying," she said finally.

"I'm not, either," he admitted. "It's been a long time since I pursued a woman. Since I even *wanted* to pursue a woman. But I feel as if I'm ready to move on to a new chapter in my life."

Lanie looked deeply into Garrett's eyes, and she

saw genuine emotion there. Confusion and excitement warred within her heart. He was being as honest with her as he could be, she was sure of that.

Then she knew he was going to kiss her again, and that if she was going to argue, now was the time. But she wanted him to kiss her. She wanted it badly.

And so she kissed him, revelling in the sweet exploration of his mouth on hers, until Dalton put up a bawling protest. Garrett took him upstairs to rock him, as they'd planned, and when he came back down they worked together to clean up the picnic.

The evening had been a simple one, the sort of evening that a husband and wife would share—at home with their child. Only they weren't husband and wife, and Garrett was going to leave. Lanie retrieved his clothes from the dryer, and he changed.

She walked him to the door, aching with the need for him to stay, to take this night of uncharted hope one step further. She wanted to make love, to know what it would feel like to have Garrett's body pressed to hers, his soul blending with her own.

But that wouldn't be a little step, that would be a big one. She'd been reckless enough for one night. There were too many things about which she was still uncertain. And the false closeness of physical intimacy wouldn't answer her questions.

Still, heat drenched her feminine center as he stopped, turned to meet her eyes in the dark hall in front of the door. He drew her close, and she felt his own arousal burgeoning against her.

He claimed her mouth with his for a long, lazy kiss that curled her toes and sent her mind reeling. It was tender, heartbreakingly romantic. She was alarmingly light-headed by the time he released her.

"Good night," he whispered into her ear, and she stood there, hanging onto the doorjamb for dear life as he drove away.

"I love hippos. They seem so worry free. They're fat and slobby, and they just don't care." Lanie rested her head against Garrett's shoulder as they sat together on a secluded bench across from the hippo enclosure. She and Dalton had met Garrett at the zoo in Austin for the afternoon. It was over a week since their picnic. It was a weekday afternoon, and crowds at the zoo were relatively sparse.

She was in over her head, and she knew it. She was more than halfway in love with Garrett already. It wasn't her nature to hold back her feelings, but she was trying. She was afraid of feeling too much, too soon. Garrett had said he was ready to move on to a new chapter in his life, but he hadn't said anything about love and trust. She knew she was going to have to take a wait-and-see approach with their relationship—which was a lot easier to accept in her head than it was in her heart.

Some hippo-style nonchalance would come in handy for her right about now. She needed to take things slow and easy until she figured out whether or not she and Garrett had a real future. She couldn't let herself love him, not knowing if he could ever love her back. She'd been down that road before, with Ben, and she wasn't going back.

"My favorite animal when I was a kid was the lion," Garrett commented lazily beside her. He was holding Dalton against his other shoulder. The baby was sleeping.

"Ah, the king of the jungle, I could have guessed," Lanie said, tipping her head up to look at him. "You Blakemores like to be in charge, don't you?"

"And what's wrong with that?" he countered lightly. "Comes in handy in the business world."

"I'm sure it does." Lanie closed her eyes, enjoying the warm breeze as she cozied against him on the shaded bench. "Ben must have taken after his mother's side of the family. He seemed to have missed out on the Blakemore killer instinct somehow."

"Killer instinct? I prefer intense aggression."

"Intense aggression? Okay." Lanie smiled to herself, thinking that if Garrett's kisses were an example of his intense aggression, he had to be a real powerhouse in a boardroom.

The light breeze felt good on her skin, and Garrett's shoulder felt even better. She fit perfectly against him.

"I barely remember Ben's mom," Garrett said quietly. "You know, Walter was crazy about Ben's mother. She died from some sort of complication following Ben's birth.''

Lanie opened her eyes, straightened. She didn't say a word, just waited for Garrett to go on. Something about the serious note in his voice told her he was about to tell her something important, if only she would listen and understand.

''I was just five then,'' he said, ''but I remember later hearing my parents talk about how much Walter changed after that. That's when his business really took off. Of course, then my parents died and Walter ended up raising me and Ben both.''

''What was that like, going to live with Walter?'' she prompted.

A couple passed, pushing a stroller, then Garrett answered her.

''Strange, at first. I didn't know Walter very well. And he wasn't a demonstrative man. I was grieving for my parents, and I'm sure he didn't know how to deal with that. It was summertime, so he took Ben and me to the office with him a lot.''

He stared toward the hippos, but she knew he was much further away than that.

She was quiet, and he went on after a few minutes. ''Ben and I would play games, taking turns pretending to be president of the company. It gave me something to focus on, something that was completely disassociated with the life I'd led before. It was even more fascinating to me as I grew older and it stopped being a game.''

''That must have made Walter happy,'' Lanie

said carefully, realizing she was learning a lot about Garrett and not wanting to say anything that would make him close up.

"I owe Walter a huge debt for raising me," Garrett said quietly. "I admire him. I know he seems harsh and cold, but he's not without feeling. You just don't know him. I promise you, he cares about Dalton. He talks about Dalton all the time." His gaze focused in on her again. "I'm not going to pressure you about the tests, but I just want you to understand that this is just Walter's way. He doesn't wear his heart on his sleeve, but that doesn't mean he doesn't have one."

She watched his big, strong hand patting Dalton as the baby stretched, waking. There was such tenderness in the automatic gesture. She sensed the words he spoke about Walter rang just as true for himself. Garrett had been hurt by love, just like Walter. Maybe that was why he understood his uncle so well.

Was there a chance she could heal them both?

Chapter Twelve

"**I**'m sorry, Lanie, I forgot about this meeting when I offered to come help you scrape paint this afternoon," Garrett said, speaking to her from the phone in his office.

Business still made his pulse race, but that was nothing compared to what his heartbeat did when he was with Lanie. The fact that an afternoon of scraping paint off her house was something he anticipated with pleasure—and regretted passing up—said it all.

It had been over a month since they'd begun seeing each other. With Lanie busy on the weekends now that the bed-and-breakfast had reopened, they usually met during the week. Garrett had been making a habit of taking some afternoons off to meet Lanie at various places—a special showing at an art gallery, a flower show at the botanical gardens, a folk music celebration in the downtown district. Dalton loved strolling or being carried, so the activities they'd planned had worked smoothly.

He wanted to be alone with her, though. He wanted it so much, he burned up inside just thinking about it. He wasn't disappointed about missing their date in Deer Creek tonight because he liked to scrape paint.

"Oh, don't worry about helping me with the house," Lanie told him, but he was glad to hear there was disappointment in her voice, too. "I'll be fine on my own."

"Why don't you just wait until another time, when I can be there?" he suggested.

"That's all right. I don't need your—"

"—help," Garrett filled in, and they both laughed. Of course she wouldn't agree to wait for him before she started working on the house, but he hadn't expected she would. And he respected her independence. She might look like a fragile flower, but she didn't act like one.

"I know you don't need my help," he said teasingly. "But do you need me?"

"Need you?" she repeated, her voice softening.

"I want to be alone with you, Lanie. No crowds. Just you and me."

The line was silent for a few seconds. "I want that, too," she whispered across the miles.

"I want to plan another picnic," he said. "Another *private* picnic, at your house. You can meet me at the door in that little gown again, and after Dalton goes to bed…''

"After Dalton goes to bed, what?" she asked, sounding breathless.

He smiled. "You'll find out," he growled softly.

They set a date, and he hung up the phone a few minutes later, and rolled his chair around to face the window and the splash of afternoon sunshine washing over the city below. But he wasn't thinking about the city, or about business. He was thinking about Lanie.

He'd never wanted anyone as much as he wanted her. It was a need like none he'd ever felt for Vanessa. Looking back, he realized now that his relationship with Vanessa had been one based on duty. He'd chosen her and married her because she was suitable, not because of fiery passion. He'd loved her, though, and she'd utilized that knowledge to stomp all over him in divorce court, leaving him bitter and emotionally drained. So drained, he hadn't thought he would ever want to get involved with another woman.

But then he'd met Lanie. She made him feel hot and dizzy and reckless in a way that was powerful and new. And that was scary—because if Vanessa had been able to hurt him, how much more might Lanie be able to?

This time, he was going to keep his feelings to himself—and keep the upper hand.

He couldn't forget that there was a lot at stake, more than just his heart. Walter continued to be anxious and troubled over the issue of the testing. He'd asked Garrett more than once to press Lanie on it because she had made no response to his attorney's letters.

Garrett had refused his uncle's requests. He knew that as long as Lanie was afraid of Walter, she wouldn't go through with the testing, and he had no idea how to resolve the situation. He felt caught in the middle between two people he cared for deeply.

He swiveled away from the window, hearing his secretary enter the room.

"Mr. Blakemore—about the meeting," she began.

"Hayden!"

Lanie almost fell off her ladder when she saw her brother come around the corner of her house. He was dressed in his uniform, and so she knew he had to have come straight from the airport.

She managed not to have an accident as she made it down the ladder and barreled into his arms.

When she was done hugging him, she punched him and said, "You jerk. You and your surprises. One of these days you're going to come home by surprise and find me gone. And it'll serve you right."

"Oh, right, gone where?" Hayden teased her.

He was hard to argue with. He knew she was the biggest homebody on the planet. She'd been feeling pretty mopey, missing Garrett, and Hayden's arrival was the perfect medicine.

It was hard to believe how much she'd come to anticipate the time she spent with Garrett, how disappointing it was when it was taken away. No matter how hard she tried to take things slow, her heart just wouldn't cooperate. She knew Garrett was tired of taking things slow, too. He wanted to take their relationship another step. And she was tempted.

She wondered what her brother would think if he knew his homebody sister was about to plunge into a hot love affair. She looked at Hayden.

"Hmmph. My life is more exciting than you think," she told him mysteriously.

Hayden laughed. "Sure, Lanie. Sure." He cocked his head in the direction of the empty baby swing on the deck. "Okay, where are you hiding the little guy? I can't wait to see him."

"Sleeping. I put him in his crib. Come on, I'll give you a peek."

Lanie led the way inside the house while Hayden explained that he was on his way to a new position at a training base in Oklahoma.

Lanie gasped, stopped and turned to stare at him. "You're not going back to Germany? Oh, Hayden, I'm so glad."

"That's right. I'll be underfoot more often." He grinned at her. "But first I've got three days with nothing planned but sitting around letting my big sister wait on me hand and foot, and playing with my brand-spanking-new little nephew."

"Ha." Lanie pivoted and headed up the stairs, Hayden directly behind her. "How about three days of scraping paint off the outside of the house and changing diapers?" she teased.

Hayden groaned. "And you wonder why I never tell you in advance when I'm coming to visit. The jobs you think up for me on the spur of the moment are bad enough. I'd hate to think what you'd come up with if I gave you advance warning!"

She shushed him when they arrived in the hallway upstairs, and he peeked in at Dalton. She wouldn't let him go inside the room.

"I'm afraid he'll wake up," she whispered. "Believe me, you'll get plenty of time to see him awake in the next three days. Never wake a baby!"

It was a Wednesday, and as usual during the weekdays, she didn't have guests. She was doing pretty good business on the weekends since she'd reopened, but her weekdays rarely filled up.

Hayden brought in his things and she set him up in one of the guest rooms. He changed clothes and joined her outside again. Dalton woke up, and she brought him out into the fresh air to meet his uncle.

They sat down together in the glider. Hayden held Dalton warily in one arm, his other casually slung around the back of the glider. Lanie leaned against his shoulder, just enjoying being together.

"You know," Hayden said after a few minutes, "I swear he looks like that baby picture of me that Gran always kept by her bed. Except for the hair. I didn't have all this dark hair."

"You had *no* hair," Lanie reminded him, toeing the glider gently to keep the motion going.

"Neither did you, so I wouldn't talk," Hayden jabbed. "Seriously, he looks like me, don't you think? You are one lucky dude," he said teasingly to Dalton.

Lanie laughed. "Okay, you have such an ego, I hated to point it out, but yes, he looks exactly like you." She leaned over impulsively to kiss him on the cheek. "I'm so glad you're here."

As she settled back, she saw a flash of color from the corner of her eye. She turned her head and saw Garrett standing at the corner of the house, one hand on the gate. He was dressed in black denim shorts and a red T-shirt.

"Garrett!" She jumped up, flew down the deck steps and rushed over to him. "Hi. What happened? Was your meeting canceled?"

"It was rescheduled at the last minute," he said stiffly. His eyes were dark, wary. "I thought you were going to be working on the house. I thought it would be all right if I came on over."

Lanie took in his rigid features, his closed expression. His coldness had an immediate dampening effect on her excitement. What was wrong?

"I *was* working on the house," she started, still breathless from her dash across the lawn, "but—"

"I didn't mean to interrupt anything," he went on, his tone formal. "I didn't realize you would have made other plans. I'm sorry. I should have phoned first."

Lanie stared at him, blinked. "What? I didn't make other plans. What do you mean?" She shot out the questions, incredulous. Then just as quickly it hit her—and hit her hard. She drew in a sharp breath. "Just what do you think you're interrupting?"

He didn't say anything, his gaze moving beyond her. She turned, saw her brother walking up with Dalton in his arms.

"Hello," Hayden said, eyeing Garrett.

"This is Garrett Blakemore, Ben's cousin." Lanie introduced the two men, her mind reeling with hurt and confusion. "This is my brother, Hayden McCall." She saw the startled flash in Garrett's eyes, and the confirmation of her instinct deepened her pain. She controlled her voice with effort, spoke quietly. "Hayden, I need to speak to Garrett alone for a few minutes, all right? Would you mind taking Dalton inside?"

Hayden looked reluctant, but nodded. He watched Garrett, and she knew her brother sensed the strange tension when he said purposefully, "I'll be right inside if you need me."

Lanie waited till Hayden and Dalton were inside, then looked back at Garrett. "I can't believe that you thought for one minute that I was with another man," she clipped out, her voice low, anger thick in her throat. She needed the anger, clung to it. Because without it, there was only pain. "I told you weeks ago that I wasn't seeing anyone, and since then you and I—" She broke off, swallowed thickly. "That *is* what you were thinking, wasn't it?" she went on. "You arrived unexpectedly, saw me with a man and you jumped to conclusions. You thought it was just like when you caught your wife cheating on you, right?"

A muscle worked in Garrett's jaw. His eyes filled with a dark torture, no longer cold. "What do you expect?" he demanded, his eyes blazing defensively. "I came back here looking for you and found some man with his arm around you, then you were kissing him—" His mouth formed a tight, hard seam. "It was a natural assumption."

"I expect you to trust me, that's what I expect," she lashed back at him. "That's what a relationship, a real relationship, is about—love, trust—all those things you said belonged in fairy tales. I knew you felt that way, but when you said that you were ready to move on to a new chapter, I thought—"

She stopped, shook her head. "I was wrong. We were both wrong. You're not ready to move on." Her anger seeped away as quickly as it had risen, leaving a horrible, sick defeat in its wake.

"Moving on doesn't mean forgetting the past," Garrett retorted. "You're supposed to learn from your mistakes. That's what I did, I learned."

His voice was knotted with stress and bitterness, and in his eyes she saw pure misery. It sliced through to her marrow. She yearned to reach out to him, heal him, but she knew now she'd been wrong to ever think she could.

The only person who could heal Garrett was Garrett. It had been wrong for her to think she could heal another person, wrong for her to even try.

"You learned that putting your love and trust into someone else's hands is a risk," she said softly. "So now you keep all your love and trust locked up inside, just like Walter. Do you really want to end up like him, old and alone?"

"You don't know what you're talking about," he snapped.

She stared at him, unable to resist one last appeal. "Maybe you're right. Maybe I don't have any business telling you what you need. But I know what I need, what I want."

Moisture stung at her eyes. She bit down on her lip, determined not to cry. Not yet, anyway.

"I want love," she told him. "And I want trust. I want all those feelings you think belong in fairy tales, and I won't settle for less. I don't think you can give me any of that—ever. I won't stand in the way of your seeing Dalton, but I don't think there's any point in our continuing to explore a relationship between the two of us. Is there?"

Silence crackled between them. Garrett gazed at her in astonishment. From the time he'd first met Lanie, he'd longed to understand what she wanted. But now that he did, he realized it was too much.

She wanted all those deep, frightening emotions inside his heart—and she wanted them exposed, laid out like an open book.

He would walk away before he gave anyone that kind of power again.

"I guess not," he answered her grimly. He used a fresh burst of frustration to propel him as he whipped around and marched back to his car. He turned the key in the ignition and the car roared to life. The tires screeched as he peeled away from the curb.

Lanie was taking a lunch break from house painting when the phone rang. She was watching a soap opera in the den while she ate her sandwich. Dalton lay on a blanket at her feet, gurgling and stretching his arms and legs. She switched off the sound on the TV with the remote control, her heartbeat doing an immediate nervous skitter at the sound of Garrett's voice on the line. Hurt coiled around her stomach.

She'd been telling herself that everything had turned out for the best, that if Garrett wasn't truly ready to move on, it was just as well she found out now. And she'd been telling herself that time would fade the pain.

But though she was still certain the first pronouncement was true, she knew now that the second one wasn't. His voice brought the pain back at full power despite the two weeks that had elapsed since their confrontation.

He didn't take time for pleasantries, went straight to the point.

"Walter's in the hospital."

Lanie gasped. "What happened?"

"He had a heart attack." Garrett's words were cold, clipped.

"I'm sorry," she said automatically but sincerely. Walter was Dalton's grandfather, no matter what. She'd never wished the old man ill.

There was a part of her that still hoped she could find a way to bring Dalton and Walter together, a way that wouldn't feel so threatening. She realized with a shock that she'd always assumed there would be plenty of time for that.

Maybe she'd been wrong.

"How is he?" she asked quickly. "Is he going to be all right?"

"He needs surgery. But he's insisting on one thing first. He wants to see Dalton."

Lanie drew in another gasp, conflicted emotions rushing through her. She felt terrible that Walter was ill. But at the same time it seemed as if he was using the crisis to make yet another of his demands, and it made her angry—because this demand she couldn't refuse.

And that was what Walter was counting on. He finally had her cornered. She'd wanted to bring Dalton and his grandfather together eventually, but she'd wanted it to be on her own terms.

"How serious is the surgery?" she asked with a tentative voice.

"It's *surgery,* Lanie. It's serious. It's a bypass operation."

She was silent for a long stretch of time.

"All right," she said at last. "I'll bring Dalton.

Tell me what hospital, what floor to meet you on,
and I'll be there as soon as I can.''

Garrett gave her the information and abruptly
hung up the phone.

Lanie set the phone down and stared at it for
several chilling seconds, dread washing over her.
Whether she liked it or not, she was about to let
Walter Blakemore into her son's life.

And whether her heart could stand it or not, she
was about to see Garrett again. The thought made
her feel weak all the way to her knees.

But what choice did she have?

She took Dalton upstairs. She dressed him in one
of his Sunday-best outfits and changed her own
clothes. Grabbing Dalton's diaper bag, she went out
to the car and headed toward the city, her heart in
her throat all the way.

Chapter Thirteen

Garrett walked away from the pay phone on the wall inside the waiting room of the intensive care unit. He sat, picked up a newsmagazine, then put it back down, too restless to read.

He was worried about Walter, but it was more than that. Hearing Lanie's voice hurt terribly, more than he'd expected. He'd thought he was ready, steeled. Then she'd picked up the phone, and he'd felt such a heartsick craving, it had made his whole chest ache.

He didn't want to crave her anymore. He didn't want to dream about her, need her. But he did, and it all seemed to get worse every day instead of better.

She'd sounded as unhappy as he felt. There had been a sadness in her voice he hadn't heard before.

Hearing his voice hurt her, too—but there was no satisfaction in that for him. Only a deep regret he didn't know how to resolve.

And he'd done nothing but rack his mind for some way to resolve it, ever since the day he'd walked away from her. She wanted him to tell her he loved her, trusted her. And before Vanessa, he could have done that. But how did he know that what he was feeling for Lanie was even real? He'd thought it was real once before, and it had turned out to be a painful fraud.

Lanie wanted such a gigantic leap of faith from him. He'd made that leap before and had suffered the consequences. It made him agitated just thinking about doing it again, making himself that vulnerable to another person. He'd been working fifteen- and twenty-hour days trying to ease the pain of it. He'd buried himself in the comfortable world of his work.

But it didn't seem as comfortable anymore. It seemed incomplete. He'd been driving in to work, only the day before, his mind trained on the intricacies of a business deal he was working on, when a commercial on the radio had speared into his consciousness. It had been a commercial for the fair, and his immediate thought had been that he would have liked to take Lanie and Dalton.

He closed his eyes, rubbing at his forehead as if he could banish her from his mind that way. But he couldn't, and a minute later he rose, started pacing, because he didn't know how else to work off the restless energy roiling inside his heart.

The downtown Austin hospital was huge and busy. Lanie pushed Dalton's stroller through a set of double glass doors and entered a large atrium-style lobby. She was sure the atmosphere had been created to soothe, with sunshine pouring down from skylights and the overgrowth of plants to absorb the murmur of voices.

But she wasn't soothed. Nerves skittered up her spine as she crossed the lobby to one of the banks of elevators. Inside, she pressed the button for the fourth floor, where Garrett had told her to meet him. The elevator car whisked noiselessly upward. She was concerned about the meeting with Walter—and Garrett.

She saw him as soon as the elevator doors opened. He was standing at the end of the hall, deep in conversation with a doctor. Her heart contracted as she stepped out of the elevator, soaking in the sight of him. He was wearing a dark suit with a white shirt and red tie. He looked perfect, as always, but even from this distance she could see the tension on his face. She wanted to go to him, but she was afraid to.

She walked up to the nurses' station instead.

"Can you tell me how Walter Blakemore is doing?" she asked the nurse on the other side of the counter. She was an older woman, with a cheerful expression and curious eyes.

"Mr. Blakemore? He's awaiting surgery. Are you a relative?" The nurse lifted her brows.

"Uh, yes. Well, I'm the mother of his grandson."

The nurse's eyes narrowed. "Aha." She stood and leaned over the counter. "So that's the grandson. We've heard about him. Isn't he a cutie?"

Lanie wondered if Walter had really put it that way, referred to Dalton as his grandson.

She looked down the hall and saw Garrett heading toward her. The doctor accompanied him.

The pit of stress in her stomach swelled.

"Thank you for coming," Garrett said when he reached her, his dark irises revealing nothing of his thoughts.

He made the necessary introductions. Dr. Johnston was a tall, lean man with a kind face and an efficient air.

"And this is the fellow all the fuss is about, eh?" Dr. Johnston said, bending to tap the baby on the nose.

"How is Walter?" Lanie asked. She directed her question at the doctor, but she could feel Garrett's hard gaze on her, feel the tension. It was horrible, standing so close to him and trying so hard not to love him. She wanted to offer him her support, her concern, but she didn't know if he'd accept it.

Dr. Johnston straightened as he answered her. "Fortunately his general health is good," he said. "There's risk with all surgery, of course. Especially surgery of this kind. But if all goes well, he should sail through this and look forward to a complete recovery."

"Good." Lanie felt some measure of relief. "All right. Should I take Dalton in to see him now?"

The doctor nodded. "Yes. He's been quite insistent about seeing this boy. We've got him scheduled for surgery this afternoon, so if you'll come this way." He led Lanie down the hall, toward double doors leading into the intensive care unit.

The doctor pushed open the door and stood there. She looked at Garrett.

"Let's go," he said quietly. "Walter's waiting for you."

And for just a second she thought she saw something in his eyes, a flash of feeling, but then it was gone and she wasn't sure if it was anything to do with her at all, or simply something to do with Walter.

She took a deep breath. Dr. Johnston pushed the doors open, and with Garrett at her side she stepped inside the ICU.

Dr. Johnston left them outside Walter's room. She leaned down to unstrap Dalton from his stroller and pick him up. The delay gave her one last chance to gather her courage. She straightened and stared at the door, Dalton in her arms.

It was silly to be this scared, she told herself finally. Walter was just a man, a human being. She'd made him into something huge in her mind, something powerful and monstrous.

"Lanie?" Garrett prompted.

She took a deep breath, looked up at him and nodded. He pushed open the door to the private room and ushered her inside.

Walter was sitting up in the bed, surrounded by a confusing array of machinery. He looked ill, pale. Still, he exuded a strong presence through his dark, cold eyes that pinned her as she walked into the room. He was an older version of Ben and Garrett, his features hard and lined. He had thick, white hair and it was as well-groomed as if he were in a boardroom. She almost expected to look down and find him wearing a suit instead of the light-colored hospital gown.

"Hi," she said softly, very uncertain of what to say or do. She held Dalton close instinctively, knowing she was about to share him with his grandfather and still uncomfortable with what that was going to mean to all their lives.

Walter watched her, his eyes set deep in his ashen face. "This is the boy?" He shifted his attention to Dalton.

Lanie swallowed tightly, nodded. She forced herself to step closer.

"Yes, this is Dalton." She felt herself sweating, intimidated despite Walter's obvious physical incapacity. She looked back and saw Garrett still standing near the door, his arms crossed, watching her.

"I want you to bring the boy over here," Walter ordered gruffly. "I can't get a good look at him from across the room."

Lanie walked to his bedside. She watched Walter's face, the way he examined Dalton.

"He doesn't look like Ben," he announced finally, his tone implying some huge fault.

"He looks a lot like my brother," Lanie told him, her back stiffening.

She stood there, feeling awkward and afraid—and then suddenly angry at Walter for making her feel that way. Angry for the critical way he was regarding her baby. Angry for everything he'd held back from Ben—and was now holding back from Dalton.

And angry because of whatever emotional influence the old man had had on Garrett, for the love he hadn't given to him, either.

She let the fury carry her. "Why did you ask me to bring Dalton here?"

Walter's hard gaze zeroed in on her again. He didn't answer her, posed his own question instead.

"Why won't you have the testing done to prove this boy is Ben's?" he demanded.

"Is that why you asked me to come, to badger me about the testing?"

"There's a lot at stake here, young lady," he said, his cheeks flushing with spots of color. "If this boy is proven to be Ben's child, he's the heir to a fortune. You have no idea—"

"I don't want to have any idea." She faced Walter squarely, unblinkingly. "I don't want to know anything about your fortune. Neither did Ben."

"Ben didn't know what he wanted."

"Yes, he did," she said, keeping her voice low, controlled. "He wanted his father to love him and accept him."

A muscle ticked in Walter's jaw. His mouth tightened and his eyes hollowed. "You don't know what you're talking about," he growled.

"I know exactly what I'm talking about. You think you can use your money to control everyone around you. Well, it didn't work with Ben. And it's not going to work with me—or my baby."

And she realized that she'd been right, that he was just a man, just a human being—and a sad shell of a human being at that. He could try to run Dalton's life, but she wouldn't let him. She was stronger than he was.

A sense of calm washed over her.

"You'll have those tests or Dalton won't see a dime of my money," Walter snapped at her. "Are you going to take that away from him?"

"I'm not taking anything away from Dalton. You are. And I'm not talking about money, either. You're taking away from him the same thing you took away from Ben. Ben is dead now."

She saw him flinch, but that didn't stop her. She kept on going—for Ben and for Dalton. "Now you're afraid you're going to die. Are you ever going to figure out what matters?"

Tension crackled between them. Neither of them spoke for a long moment.

"You wanted to see Dalton, I brought him. And

I'm glad I came. I was scared of you before—and now I'm not. All I feel for you is pity."

She turned away. Garrett was staring at her, his face strained with a shuttered emotion she couldn't decode. She wasn't sure if it was anger…or pain.

"Wait," Walter ordered harshly from behind her.

She froze, something in his voice, something painful, forcing her to turn. He looked small, dwarfed by the high-tech machinery all around him.

"What?"

He stared at her for a long time. His eyes looked bright suddenly, very bright.

"I want to hold him," he said gruffly. "Bring him over here and let me hold him."

His words were demanding, but there was a pleading in his tone, in his eyes.

Her first instinct was to refuse, to keep right on walking out of the room. He didn't deserve to hold Dalton. But she couldn't walk away.

She took Dalton back to him and held him out to his grandfather wordlessly. Walter took the baby into his arms. He didn't say anything, just held Dalton for a long moment, touching his face, his hands. She noticed that his fingers shook, and she noticed how closely and tenderly he held the baby.

Then he handed Dalton back. Lanie took him, and as she did, she saw the moisture that welled up in his grandfather's eyes. She remembered what Garrett had said about Walter having a heart despite how harsh and cold he seemed on the outside.

Her throat felt thick suddenly, sorrow overwhelming her.

"I know that you love him," she said softly, desperately controlling the shake in her voice. "You know he's your grandson, and you love him. You loved Ben, too, I know you did."

Walter didn't answer, looked away, his mouth tight but trembling. He crossed his arms and she noticed that they were thin and pale, and she wanted so desperately to reach out and touch his hand that she had to clench her fist at her side to stop from doing it. She wasn't sure how he'd react if she touched him.

"You have a grandson now," she whispered. "You can't do anything about the past, but you can change the future—if you want to." As she ended, she turned, her gaze locking with Garrett's.

And she reminded herself that she couldn't heal Walter any more than she could heal Garrett. She'd said what was in her heart. She was finished.

The old man didn't respond to her comments. He was still staring at the wall when she left.

Garrett followed her into the hall. He closed Walter's door softly behind them.

Lanie tucked Dalton back into his stroller, then straightened and looked Garrett in the eye. She'd made a decision, and it seemed appropriate that he should be the first to hear.

"I've decided to go ahead with the blood and DNA testing."

Chapter Fourteen

Garrett paced the hall outside the ICU.

Hours had passed since Lanie's confrontation with Walter. She was gone now, gone home to Deer Creek with Dalton. Walter was in recovery, awaiting transfer to a regular hospital room. He'd made it through the surgery with flying colors, according to his doctor.

The old man would be happy to hear the news that Lanie had decided to go through with the testing that would confirm Dalton was his grandson.

Walter had won.

But Garrett couldn't shake from his heart the sense that Walter had really *lost.* And he wasn't the only one. Garrett had lost, too.

You can't do anything about the past, but you can change the future—if you want to. Lanie's words echoed over and over in his mind.

He knew she hadn't just meant those words for Walter. She'd meant them for him, too.

But wasn't that what he'd been trying to do? He'd once given his love and trust freely, openly. Now he was proceeding with more prudence. What kind of fool would repeat the same mistake twice?

If he gave Lanie what she wanted, he could end up in exactly the same situation he'd been in with Vanessa. He could end up hurting and alone.

Garrett stopped short at the end of the hall. He was hurting and alone *now,* wasn't he? He'd turned his back on Lanie, but that hadn't made him hurt any less.

If he gave her what she wanted, he was taking a huge risk. But if he didn't, he was dooming himself to the very future he was trying to avoid. And he would risk passing up a chance at true happiness. Just because it had been a mistake in the past didn't have to mean it was a mistake now.

I've decided to go ahead with the blood and DNA testing.

Cold fingers wrapped around his heart, and he realized why he was so uncomfortable with her decision to have Dalton undergo the testing—because it took away his choice. He'd had a choice about offering his faith to her before, and now it was gone. She wasn't asking for his faith anymore.

He was too late.

She'd given up on him.

Lanie walked the floors, back and forth, singing softly to Dalton. He was unusually fussy. It had been a tense day, with their unexpected trip into Austin and the confrontation in Walter's hospital room. She hoped that was all that was bothering Dalton, and that he wasn't flirting with colic.

She was feeling pretty disturbed herself. The calm that had fallen over her in Walter's room had receded into a lingering melancholy. She was glad the encounter was behind her—it was something she'd known was coming, eventually. But her triumph in facing Walter was overpowered by the deep sense of loss that came with seeing Garrett.

She couldn't kick the hope that it wasn't too late for them, that Garrett could learn to love and trust again—*if he wanted to.*

She sniffled, reaching up to dash a traitorous tear before it spilled down her cheek. She was too romantic. It had gotten her in trouble before, and she was surely in deep water now. She wanted to turn Garrett into a knight in shining armor, riding up on a white charger to declare his undying devotion—just like in one of the fairy tales he had accused her of believing in. No doubt her grandmother had read her too many fanciful stories as a child.

Garrett wasn't going to come riding up. She needed to get over it, she chastised herself sternly.

Dalton's fussing turned to flat-out bawling just then.

"You're not happy, either, are you, sweetie?" she murmured. She checked his diaper again, then tried to feed him again, but he wasn't wet or hungry. He didn't have a temperature. Why was he so cranky? He'd been increasingly out of sorts all evening.

Lanie felt like crying herself. Patting and jiggling him, she went upstairs to rummage through her baby guidebook for a clue to her son's behavior.

"Okay, you're probably too old to be getting colicky now," she decided, scanning the book. "Thank goodness." Dalton was a lively baby, but not a regular crier. "Early teething. Hmm."

She used his next howl to check his mouth and saw a speck of white erupting from his lower gum. It was barely visible, and she wasn't surprised she hadn't noticed it before.

"Aha."

She studied the book for a few more minutes, deciding to follow the medicate-then-distract plan.

She could use some distraction herself. A few minutes later, after giving Dalton a dose of infant liquid acetaminophen and rubbing his gums with a teething gel, she congratulated herself on a well-stocked medicine cabinet and set off for a walk. It was a warm summer evening, still light out, and the baby book promised a stroll in fresh air was a sure-fire mood enhancer for fussy babies.

A once-around-the-block had a miraculous effect. Strapped in his stroller, Dalton quieted, seemingly entranced by the chirping of birds in the trees and the hum of the occasional car passing by. On the second trip around the block, even Lanie started to feel a little better. She'd needed the fresh air, too. Sunset deepened into dusk, and the soft light soothed her frazzled nerves. Dalton had been lulled into sleep by the time she rounded the corner of her street.

Her stomach quivered when she saw a luxury vehicle parked in front of her house. It looked exactly like Garrett's car.

But it couldn't be.

She pushed the stroller a little faster, her heart pounding.

Garrett spotted her in his rearview mirror. He opened the car door and stood.

She stopped, staring at him from the sidewalk. Her lips parted slightly and her eyes widened in an expression of utter astonishment. Her gold hair hung free around her shoulders, bared by the sleeveless white top she wore over jean shorts.

"What are you doing here?" she asked after a long, silent beat. Then concern flashed across her face. "Is it Walter? Did something happen? Did he—?"

"No," he rushed to assure her. "Walter's fine. He sailed through the surgery and is expected to make a full recovery." He walked around the car to join her on the sidewalk. He noticed Dalton sleeping in his stroller. "That's not why I'm here." He hesitated, not sure how to go on, only knowing he had to find the words. His future depended on it. "I got here a few minutes ago, but you weren't home, so I decided to wait."

"I took Dalton out for a walk," Lanie said, still

looking at him blankly. "He's cutting his first tooth and he was really grouchy. Luckily the walk seems to have done the trick."

"Can you get him out of the stroller without waking him up?" Garrett asked.

She blinked. "I don't know. I wasn't thinking that far ahead."

"How would you feel about a fresh pair of arms to rock him to sleep if he wakes up when you get him inside?" he asked.

Lanie tilted her head, stared at him suspiciously. "You didn't come all the way out here to find out if I needed help getting Dalton to sleep," she commented sensibly.

"You're right."

"Do you mind if we walk?" he suggested. "I have something to tell you."

She nodded. "Okay." Dalton started moving in his seat, his little mouth curving into a big yawn, his eyelids fluttering. "Looks like Dalton could use another trip around the block, anyway."

They moved forward together, Lanie pushing the stroller, Garrett keeping pace beside her. Dalton fell asleep again.

Garrett didn't say anything for the first few minutes, and she sneaked a peek at his profile. He looked lost in thought, his features hard, shuttered. Then he looked at her, and she saw his eyes weren't hard and shuttered at all. They were filled with an emotion she couldn't begin to decipher.

She wished he would speak. Not knowing why

he'd come was almost unbearable. She was hoping... And she didn't want to hope.

It was too painful.

"Imagine you're in a relationship," he began slowly, his voice low, serious. He was staring straight ahead as he walked. "You're in love, or at least you think you are. And you think she's in love with you, too. Everything seems perfect—until one day you come home, walk into your bedroom and your heart is ripped out of your chest."

"Oh, Garrett." She stopped the stroller, not sure what to say, how to respond to the pain in his voice. She already knew what had happened in his marriage, and hearing it again wouldn't change anything. "You don't have to explain—"

"Yes, I do." He kept walking, and she caught up with him. "Imagine you withdraw. You keep your feelings inside, locked up, safe. And you do it for so long that it's not even a conscious thing anymore. It's just a way of life. Or more accurately, a way of *not* living."

Garrett stopped and stared at Lanie. She was watching silently, so he took a deep breath and kept going.

"Then one day you meet someone who starts picking at those locks," he continued. "They make you feel, and it's scary and painful. But you *want* to feel, because when it's not scary and painful, it's bright and wonderful, alive and real."

"Garrett—" A tear slid down Lanie's cheek.

"Let me finish." He reached out, captured the

tear with his thumb. "You asked me if I wanted to end up like Walter. I don't. I really don't." He cupped her face in his hands, stared straight into her shimmering eyes. "I love you, Lanie," he whispered roughly. "I love you, and I trust you. I want to feel everything you make me feel. Tell me it's not too late for me to tell you that. Tell me it still matters."

"Of course it matters," she exclaimed, her voice thick with emotion. "It's all that matters."

He closed his eyes briefly in relief, in silent thanks. Then opened them to gaze on her dear face.

"I love you," he repeated. "I want to tell you that every day, until you're so sick of it that you beg me to stop."

"I'd never do that," she promised, tears tracking down both cheeks.

He slid his arms down to her waist. She let go of the push bar of the stroller and buried herself in his embrace—holding him, just holding him, and loving him as he held her back. She could hear the frantic pounding of his heart, keeping time with her own.

"I love you!" he shouted out for all the world to hear when he pulled back, shaking off the shackles of his fear once and for all.

She laughed through her tears. "I love you, too, but you're going to wake up Dalton," she pointed out.

Dalton made a little mewl then, stretching and

opening his eyes. His face brightened when he spotted Garrett, and he reached his chubby arms up.

"He wants you," Lanie said.

Garrett unbuckled the baby from the stroller and lifted him up. "I love your mommy," he told Dalton.

Then he shot a quick glance at Lanie.

"Excuse me," Garrett said. "I have to ask Dalton something."

Lanie lifted a brow.

"Dalton, seeing as how you're the closest male relative, and I want to do it all up proper, I'd like to request your mother's hand in marriage. Is that all right with you, bud?"

Dalton gurgled.

Garrett's soft, tender gaze moved to Lanie. Happiness danced up and down her spine.

"I think it's okay with the little guy," Garrett said. With the baby braced in the crook of one arm, he knelt down right there on the sidewalk. "Lanie, will you marry me?"

"Yes," she breathed, her eyes alight with the kind of joy that lasted forever.

Garrett rose and pulled her into his arms again, baby and all. He found her mouth, claiming it and her with all the passion of true love.

And they would have stayed that way a lot longer if Dalton hadn't put up a squealing protest.

"Timing, boy," Garrett scolded him lightly. "I've got to teach you about timing...."

Epilogue

Lanie stared at her reflection in the gilded mirror of the dressing room. The white lace gown she wore was nothing short of magical—as was everything else in her life.

She looked—and felt—like a princess, and not because she was getting married in the most majestic cathedral in Austin. Not even because Garrett had arranged for them to be whisked away in a horse-drawn carriage afterward. She felt like a princess because she was in love, and this time she was truly loved in return.

It had been two months since Garrett's proposal. He'd been in a rush to marry, but he'd insisted on taking the time to design the fairy-tale wedding he insisted she deserved. She knew he'd hired a fleet of wedding planners to pull it off, and she loved him all the more for it. But she looked forward to the simple life they intended to lead in Deer Creek following the ceremony—with her bed-and-breakfast, her baby and her new husband. Garrett was already planning and adjusting his work schedule to fit the new life they would build together.

"Lanie! It's time!" She heard Patty calling from outside the door of her dressing room. Lanie pulled Dalton away from her breast. He gave her a milky smile. Adjusting her gown into place after the last-minute feeding, she rose, smoothing the ornate dress as she gave it one last check in the mirror, and walked to the door. Butterflies skipped inside her when she thought of all the people waiting in the church sanctuary, all the eyes that would soon be upon her.

Walter stood in the hall, his face hard as ever but his eyes soft as they landed on his grandson. The test results had provided the evidence he'd required, but he hadn't ever said another word to Lanie about his money. She wondered if her words to him that day in his hospital room had found a home in his heart, but she didn't expect him to ever say so. It was enough that he'd come to the wedding. It was enough that he wanted to hold his grandson through the ceremony. Lanie knew that love took its own time, found its own way.

Walter sat down in the back of the church and, after a quick flurry of activity and organizing, Patty marched up the aisle as matron of honor. Hayden took Lanie's arm, and she looked toward the altar, the sea of guests blurring on the periphery of her vision. Her very own Prince Charming awaited her—his face aglow with pure love, complete trust and undiluted happiness. Her nervousness dissolved. She felt sure, steady.

She saw the future in his eyes, and she stepped toward it with wonder and awe.

* * * * *

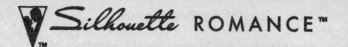
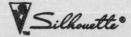

SILHOUETTE BOOKS
is proud to announce the arrival of

THE BABY OF THE MONTH CLUB:

the latest installment of author
Marie Ferrarella's
popular miniseries.

When pregnant Juliette St. Claire met Gabriel Saldana than she discovered he wasn't the struggling artist he claimed to be. An undercover agent, Gabriel had been sent to Juliette's gallery to nab his prime suspect: Juliette herself. But when he discovered her innocence, would he win back Juliette's heart and convince her that he was the daddy her baby needed?

Don't miss Juliette's induction into
THE BABY OF THE MONTH CLUB
in September 1999.
Available at your favorite retail outlet.

Coming this September 1999
from SILHOUETTE BOOKS
and bestselling author

RACHEL LEE

ONARD
OUNTY:

Boots &
Badges

Alicia Dreyfus—a desperate woman on the run—
is about to discover that she *can* come home
again...to Conard County. Along the way she
meets the man of her dreams—and brings together
three other couples, whose love blossoms beneath
the bold Wyoming sky.

Enjoy four complete, **brand-new** stories in one
extraordinary volume.

Available at your favorite retail outlet.

Silhouette ROMANCE™

VIRGIN BRIDES

Your favorite authors tell more heartwarming stories of lovely brides who discover love... for the first time....

July 1999 GLASS SLIPPER BRIDE
Arlene James (SR #1379)

Bodyguard Jack Keller had to protect innocent Jillian Waltham—day and night. But when his assignment became a matter of temporary marriage, would Jack's hardened heart need protection...from Jillian, his glass slipper bride?

September 1999 MARRIED TO THE SHEIK
Carol Grace (SR #1391)

Assistant Emily Claybourne secretly loved her boss, and now Sheik Ben Ali had finally asked her to marry him! But Ben was only interested in a temporary union...until Emily started showing him the joys of marriage—and love....

November 1999 THE PRINCESS AND THE COWBOY
Martha Shields (SR #1403)

When runaway Princess Josephene Francoeur needed a short-term husband, cowboy Buck Buchanan was the perfect choice. But to wed him, Josephene had to tell a few white lies, which worked...until "Josie Freeheart" realized she wanted to love her rugged cowboy groom forever!

Available at your favorite retail outlet.

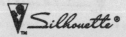